MW01094360

RUBY - RED SLIPPERS AND ALL

by

Iris Bolling

Printed in the United States of America

ISBN- 9780991342662

Library of Congress Control Number: 2015921268

This is a work of fiction. Names, characters, places and incidents are with the product of the author's imagination or are used fictitiously, and any resemblance to actual persons, living or dead, business establishments, events, locales is entirely coincidental.

SIRI ENTERPRISES
RICHMOND, VIRGINIA
www.siriaustin.com
www.irisbolling.net

Books By Iris Bolling
The Heart Series

Once You've Touched The Heart
The Heart of Him
Look Into My Heart
A Heart Divided
A Lost Heart
The Heart

Night of Seduction Series

Night of Seduction/Heaven's Gate
The Pendleton Rule

Gems and Gents Series

Teach Me
The Book of Joshua I – Trust
The Book of Joshua II – Believe
A Lassiter's Christmas
Ruby...Red Slippers & All
The Book of Adam: HYPNOTIC

Brooks Family Values Series

Sinergy
Fatal Mistake
Propensity For Love

CHAPTER ONE

"Good evening Joe," Devin Upton spoke as he opened the door to the warehouse office.

"Hello Devin. Thank you for staying late. We have documents that need your signature to change the shipping accounts from your father's name to yours."

Devin took a seat at his warehouse manager's conference table and began signing documents. "How is the family, Joe?"

"The family is fine," Joe replied as he accepted the first document and glanced over it. "I'm sure your mother is excited to have you home for good."

"Joe, may I ask you a question." Devin stopped writing and looked up. "How has she been? Honestly?"

"Well, son, I'm just the warehouse manager. I don't see her every day."

"My Dad used to tell me if you want to know what's happening in the building, ask Joe," Devin smiled. "He may not talk much, but he treats every employee like family. And he was right. You are one of the reasons I felt comfortable leaving to take care of matters when Dad died. I knew you would check in on my Mother."

"Your mother is a remarkable woman. There were days when she was down and I was a bit concerned. But your calls kept her spirits up," Joe replied. "I have to say, I miss your father. We had some good talks right here at this table."

Devin looked off as Joe talked. He never really took the time to talk with his dad. They had a good relationship, but most of his father's time was spent at the office when he was young. Then he was off to Harvard, where they had their Sunday calls that consisted of the newest business developments, stocks, bonds, but never anything personal. He had no doubt his father had loved him, but it was his mother who had taken him to little league baseball games, the parent teacher conferences and who was the one who had the mother son talk, versus the father son talk. He'd had his first heart to heart talk with his dad ten days before he died. He came home after his mother called. She was upset. She had finally gotten his father to get a exam, but it was too late. His father was given less than a month to live. It turned out to be ten days. They talked more in that time than they had his entire life. Devin's father told him about his grandmother. How she was a single mother who had moved from shelter to shelter to make sure Devin's dad had a bed to sleep in and at least one hot meal a day. She would take him to school then spend the day selling her body to take care of him. She died right after Devin's dad graduated from high school. To honor her, he'd worked two jobs, gotten an efficiency apartment and put himself through college. He lived in that apartment for ten years, until he met Devin's mother. He had made several small investments that had done well, but Miranda did not care. She loved him unconditionally. Soon after they married, he started Upton Investments. Twenty years later they were one of the wealthiest families in the country. They continued to live modestly with neighbors who had no idea they lived next door to millionaires. Devin had had no idea how wealthy his parents were until his father's attorney spoke with him after the funeral. For the last six months, Devin had been closing his father's many accounts trying to determine a final dollar amount for his estate. Between bank accounts, stocks, bonds and property, his mother would never want for anything. Now he had one promise left to fulfill. His father wanted to give homeless families the chance his mother had not received. Devin's plan was to make certain their foundation accomplished just that.

Joe studied the thirty-eight year old. The younger man was six-two and a darker version of his father. Joe thought he would surely make some pretty grand babies one day. "You okay, Son?"

Devin looked up. "Yes, yes, sorry about that, I was lost in thought."

Joe laughed as he took the last set of papers. "Your dad used to do that when he came up with new ideas."

"Do what?" Devin called out to him.

"Get lost in thoughts. Then he would walk out that door and the next thing I knew something big would happen."

"I have big shoes to fill," Devin sat back. "I'm not the same as my father. I have book sense where he knew how to get his hands dirty."

Joe stood and poured both of them a cup of coffee. Young Upton was more like his father than he knew. When Aaron needed to talk he would sit at that table with him and just listen.

"You've been here since the beginning of Upton Investments."

Joe sat the cup in front of Devin. "Over thirty years. The company has been good to me. I've raised twelve children working here."

"Big family," Devin drank from his cup. "How did he do it Joe? How did he keep the company strong for so many years?"

Joe smiled. "Your father always cared about people like family. It didn't matter if they lived on the big hill with the gated communities or down the hill where there is a liquor store on every corner. He treated people like they mattered. He listened to people and would make decisions based on what he heard."

"You know I always wondered why he never set up a board. A team of people to help with the decision making."

Joe laughed, a deep rich laugh. "He used to say too many people could screw up a wet dream. Too many barriers to the desired outcome."

Devin looked up from the document laughing. "It's hard to screw up a wet dream."

"Not according to your father. He said every opinion added a week to getting an answer on how to reach a peak. If you know what I mean," Joe laughed then took a drink. "In the time it would take a board to meet and make a decision Aaron said he could have screwed every woman in the building. In his sleep, that is." Joe nodded thinking about the loss of his friend. "He trusted his gut and Miranda when it came to making decisions for this company."

"He had my mother. Now it's on me," Devin stood. "Thanks for the coffee and the ear."

Joe shook the younger man's hand. "You're the start of a new day here. Like your father, you'll find the right gem to light your way."

"From your lips to God's ears. Good night Joe," Devin said as he walked out of the office. He thought about Joe as he walked to his car. The man had worked the nightshift for as long as he could remember. When did he find time to have twelve children? He shook his head smiling as he got into his vehicle. "That man must really love his wife."

CHAPTER TWO

The last thing on Ruby Lassiter's agenda was changing a flat tire. When she woke up this morning she checked everything on her schedule and was certain there was nothing mechanical on the list. Yet here she stood, no, bent, changing a flat tire, in her red, silk blend, nothing but business, suit on. In heels that were sure to make any woman scream, "have mercy" and with rain dripping down her back from the umbrella the elderly woman was holding above her.

"Are you okay down there dear?" the woman asked out of concern.

"Yes, ma'am, It's just about done," she convincingly replied.

All of the six girls in her family knew how to change tires, oil, and fluids. Hell, if need be, with the right equipment, they could replace a motor. Between her father and six brothers, they made sure the girls knew everything about cars and how to maintain them.

"There you are ma'am." Ruby stood with the jack in her hand. "That spare tire will only hold you for a few miles. You may want to head straight for a mechanic once you leave here." She placed the jack in the trunk of the woman's vehicle.

"Please let me give you something for doing this. I'm not sure what I would have done if you had not come along."

"No, thank you. Just make sure you get that tire replaced soon, okay." Ruby looked at her watch. She was late. Some first impression she was going to make with the Board of Directors of Upton Investments. "I hate to leave you, but I'm late for an appointment. Are you sure you will be okay?"

"Yes, thank you," the woman replied. "I don't have far to go."

Ruby helped the woman into her car and then ran towards hers. Before she reached the door, an SUV drove past at a high speed and hit a puddle of water that splashed down the front of Ruby's suit.

"Great," she declared, "Not only am I going to be late, now I'm wet." As she sat in her car, a few curse words escaped her lips, "Well, they are just going to see what a wet hen looks like for real." She turned the key in the ignition and pulled off.

Satisfied that she had done all she could to make the front of her skirt presentable, Ruby took a deep breath and walked towards the conference room. When she walked through the door of one of the most exclusive hotels in the city of Richmond, she knew this was the type of place her sister Pearl or brother Joshua would frequent. Not her. She worked at Vital Statistics as a civil servant. Her salary barely covered her apartment and car note. There were no extras for something as elegant as The Jefferson Hotel. Ruby took a deep breath and opened the door to the conference room. Stepping inside, she was transformed into a different time period. The dome shape of the ceiling, with a mural depicting various periods in history astounded her. The Victorian style draperies and tapestry were absolutely beautiful, for a minute she thought she should bow or curtsy or something.

"Excuse me." A feminine voice cleared her throat, "You must be in the wrong room. Housekeeping is down the hallway to your right."

The condescending tone in the woman's voice, immediately struck a chord in Ruby. All her life people had talked down to her and her family, because they lived on the wrong side of the tracks or because her mother chose to have twelve children, so she was used to it. However, that did not mean she accepted it.

"And the ladies room is just past housing, keeping on the left. You seem a bit uptight, you may want to relieve yourself, then come back and try greeting people again."

Another young woman seated at the table chuckled, than stopped when an evil eye was sent in her direction from the first woman. Ruby smiled at the young woman.

Tania Reid, the acting Human Resources director for Upton Investments stared at the woman in the soiled clothes and with a snobbish, once over, look, turned her back on Ruby.

"This is a private meeting for Upton Investments," then she looked back, "I'm certain you were not invited."

Still not liking the tone of the woman's voice, Ruby returned the snobbish, once over, look and replied. "I hope you didn't put any money on that. You would lose the bank." She looked the woman up and down. "This is exactly where I am supposed to be."

"Now you just wait one minute, missy..."

"The name is Ruby Lassiter and you are?" Ruby simply raised an eyebrow at the woman daring her to say something else.

The woman looked at the papers on the table and saw the name listed for the Director of Aaron's House. She looked back at the woman standing there with the 'sister girl' attitude, who looked to be no more than twenty-five and could not believe her eyes. Devin had lost his mind if he thought she was going to work for a woman that did not know you do not wear red to a business meeting. "Would you mind stepping outside for a moment?"

"Look, I'm not sure what the problem is but I'm supposed to be here for a meeting concerning a homeless shelter for the downtown Richmond area, is this or is it not the right place?"

"It's the right place," another woman sitting at the conference table replied as she stood. "I'm Karin Jacobs. I represent the city in this matter." Ruby shook the hand that was extended to her. "It's nice to meet you Ms. Lassiter, your name precedes you."

"Thank you, Ms. Jacobs."

"Cecil Dance of C.D. Construction," the man sitting at the table stood and extended his hand.

Ruby shook it and smiled, "It's nice to meet you sir." She then turned to Tania, "Do you have a name that goes along with that attitude?"

"Yes, I do. We are not in need of your services. You may leave."

Ruby threw her hands up in the air, "Fine by me. I have a job." She reached into her skirt pocket, pulled out a dollar bill and placed it on the table. "Just in case they don't have enough toilet paper in the ladies room, 'cause you got a lot of shit inside of you that needs to be let out." She turned and pushed the door to walk out but collided with something or someone.

CHAPTER THREE

The grace his mother possessed always amazed him. Devin Upton, the new CEO of Upton Investments shook his head as Miranda Upton walked towards him. Anyone looking at her would think she wasn't a day over forty, which was mathematically impossible because he was thirty-eight.

"Hello mother," he lovingly kissed her on the cheek. "You look wonderful."

"Thank you dear," she palmed his cheek. "How have you been? I haven't seen you in six months, is that any way to treat your mother?"

Devin smiled lovingly at the woman he considered incredible. "You know I was busy dissecting dad's properties in the Caymans. Now that that is complete, I can concentrate on his final wish.

"Did you find someone to handle the details?'

They turned to walk towards the doors of the Jefferson Hotel conference room on the first floor. "We have two candidates from what I understand. The first one should be here. I have not met her personally, but I have it on good authority she will meet our needs."

"Good, let's give your father something that proudly carries his name."

Devin reached to open the door to the conference room to escort her inside when the door swung open. He felt the impact of the door against his hand. A pain shot up his arm as he swung around grabbing his wrist.

"Devin?" his mother called out.

Ruby gasped, "Are you okay," she asked angry that she had caused pain to someone. "I am so sorry. I didn't know someone was outside the door. She looked up and saw the Concierge walking over with a concerned look. "Would you get some ice, please?" She asked as she dropped her purse and rushed to help the man.

Devin saw the woman in the red suit and wished he could stop the pain long enough to say hello, get a number, an email anything except wince in pain.

"It's fine," he lied as pain shot through his wrist.

"Please, allow me to take a look at it," Ruby shook her head as she touched his wrist, "I'm so sorry about this. I don't think it's broken."

For a moment the pain faded with her touch. "Ouch," wrong, her attempting to bend his wrist triggered another sharp jolt though his arm. "Not good," he swallowed hard.

Suddenly they all heard a huff. "What is all this commotion?"

Ruby didn't have to turn to know it was the woman from the meeting.

"Devin!" She looked to see Ruby with Devin's hand in hers. "My lord what did you do?"

Oh lord here comes the drama, Ruby thought. A speechless Ruby searched for words, "It, it was an accident. I didn't mean to do it." She said as the woman pulled the man away from her.

"Devin, come inside the room," Tania wrapped her arms around his shoulders and directed him to the room.

The Concierge approached with the ice bag handing it to Ruby.

Tania snatched it. "I'll take that. You have caused enough damage here. You may go."

Miranda looked at the woman and recognized her immediately as the one who had stopped in the rain to help her with her flat tire.

Feeling dejected and guilty, Ruby did not respond to the blonde haired heifer with the bad dye job that was getting on her last nerve. She picked up her purse, took one look back then walked out of the door. Apparently she was not wanted or needed. The one thing Ruby never did was stay where she was not welcome. It was clear this was not the job for her.

The morning had certainly given her several warnings not to attend this meeting. "But no... you just had to come, didn't you?" She mumbled to herself as she walked out the door. "So what if it was a great opportunity to help a few families who were living on the street to find shelter from the cold?" She talked to herself while struggling with her umbrella. "Why couldn't she just let things be? Everyone else was willing to let people freeze on the street. Why did she have to be any different? The damn umbrella wouldn't stay up. Ruby threw it in the trash bin on the street. "You can go to hell too." She ran off to her vehicle.

"Wait," Miranda called out, but the woman in red was gone in the rain by the time she reached the door.

Miranda walked back to the conference room. "Tania we don't treat people in that manner," She shook her head.

Tania looked up. "Oh don't worry about her Mrs. Upton. You will not see the likes of her again."

Miranda took Devin's hand and the ice. "You call that young lady back in here. I'll handle my son."

At the moment Devin wanted everyone to stop trying to handle his arm. It was generating enough pain on its own.

"It's probably just a sprain, Mother," Devin took the ice holding it against his wrist. "I'll handle this." He took a seat. "Do you know that woman?"

"No, I don't know her, but I think she was the young lady who helped me with my car this morning."

"Your car? What happened to your car?"

"It's not important," Miranda hushed him. "Let's go on with the meeting so Tania can do as I requested." She gave the woman a stern look.

"Of course," Tania nodded. "For now we have a meeting waiting to begin."

As they all took their seats, Miranda whispered to Tania, "Find her and get her back here before the end of business today."

Tania knew not to cross Miranda. She wanted to be named head of Human Resources and Miranda pulled a lot of weight with her son. So she would do what was asked of her and call the woman back in. She could always sway Devin in a different direction when the time came. "Yes ma'am." She smiled then closed the door.

Devin sat with the ice pack on his wrist wondering if he would see those eyes again.

CHAPTER FOUR

It was the Tuesday before Thanksgiving. There were plenty of things Ruby needed to do to prepare for the family dinner and annual football challenge. The last thing she had time to do was worry about some man who didn't have the common sense to watch where he was going.

She walked through the back door of her parent's home mumbling while struggling to bring bags in the house. She placed a bag on the counter top and paused. "What if it's broken?" She shook her head then walked back out the door. She came back through with two more bags then placed them on the table. "You don't know who the man is so you can't check on him even if you wanted to." She walked back out the door. Ruby came back in with one last bag, placed it next to the others, then began removing her gloves. She stopped. "She called him Devin." She stared off into space for a long moment. Then she removed her coat hanging it on the hook next to the back door. "That's just one name. You can't call a place and just ask for

Devin. Devin who? They would ask and then what would you say?"

After watching her daughter walk back and forth in the house talking to herself, Sally, the mother to the Lassiter clan, decided she had had enough. She had been sitting at the table drinking a cup of tea when her oldest daughter came in the back door the first time. She started to speak when Ruby began talking. At first she thought Ruby was talking to her, but then she realized her child was talking to herself. Now she was curious and decided to listen.

"Okay I give. What's broke? And more interesting, what man? And who is Devin?"

A surprised Ruby turned to see her mother sitting at the table. "Oh, hey Mom. How are you today?"

And just like that the smiling Ruby was in place. "Pretty good," she said as she walked over to the bags. "You're off early today?"

"I didn't go in. I had an interview today," Ruby began removing items from the bag, placing them in the cabinets. "Are you making the cakes today for Thanksgiving dinner?"

"Ha," Sally laughed out loud. "No. They would not make it to tomorrow, much less Thursday."

Ruby laughed. "You are right. What was I thinking?"

"About a man."

"What man?" Ruby continued to put the groceries away.

"The one you were mumbling about when you walked in the door."

With a wave of her hand Ruby laughed and changed the subject. "Oh, that. It's...nothing." She turned and continued emptying the bags of groceries. "When is Phire coming home? Is she bringing her roommate with her?"

Sally noticed Ruby had changed the subject. "She will be home on Wednesday. I don't think she is getting along with her roommate too well." Sally frowned as she continued to put grocery items away. "She said the girl is uppity and has too many boys coming in and out of the room."

Ruby stopped. "I met one of those heifers today. What is it about those itty-bitty heifers who think the earth is their ground to rule and the men theirs to conquer? Walking around in itty-bitty skirts, with their hair dyed some unnatural color and fake finger nails, well-manicured like they never washed a dish in their life." She held the five-pound bag of sugar in her hands as she pointed it at Sally. "Like the world is supposed to stop and bow at their feet." She put the sugar in the cabinet with a huff. "Give me a freakin' break."

Sally stopped working, leaned over the breakfast bar with her chin braced on her hand, staring at her daughter. "The little heifer." She exclaimed.

"That's right," Ruby hefted the sugar into the cabinet. "Who is she anyway to determine if I am worthy of her little stink job? I got a job."

"That don't pay a damn," Sally added as she ate a grape from the fruit bowl."

"No they don't pay enough."

"Not to mention they work you like a dog."

"That's right." Ruby stopped. "Whom are we talking about now?"

"The job you don't need," Sally reminded her as she sat on the stool

"Yes, that's right. I don't need that job. Even though I'm the right person for it. But would that heifer know that...NO!" Ruby reached down and pulled out the twenty-five pound turkey placing it in the sink. "Know why? 'Cause the heifer didn't even let me interview. She took one look at me, frowned up her little stink ass nose and turned her back on me."

"The heifer!" Sally exclaimed.

"Who?" Ruby looked at her confused.

"I don't know. Whoever the heifer is you are talking about."

Ruby stared at her mother then the two women burst out laughing.

Sally walked over to the counter and moved the now empty bags.

"Sit." Ruby did, as Sally poured her a cup of tea. "Start from the beginning."

"Mrs. Greenwood, the Director at the shelter submitted my name for the director of a new facility due to open spring of next year. They called me in for an interview. On the way there, I stopped and helped this sweet woman with her flat tire. I got dirty, and of course it's raining outside, so I got wet. When I arrived for the interview, I truly looked like a wet hen."

"The people frowned on you because of how you looked."

"Right," Ruby took a sip of her tea. "Not all of them, just the main one."

"The heifer," Sally nodded.

"Exactly. To further infuriate the woman I left her a dollar bill and told her to use it to wipe her behind."

"I can assume you did not use those words," Sally raised an eyebrow.

Ruby blushed. "Not exactly."

Sally smiled knowingly. "And the man?"

Sitting her teacup down. "Oh, yes. When I stormed out of the room I pushed the door open and a man was standing on the other side." She threw her hands up in the air. "Of course, he got hit."

"This man was Devin?"

"I had already embarrassed myself enough. I didn't hang around long enough to find out."

CHAPTER FIVE

Devin sat at the conference table with the icepack resting on his wrist. He hoped to keep the swelling down until he could get it examined. The pain was still throbbing, but nothing he couldn't stand.

"The first order of business was to establish the Director for Aaron's House," Karin Jacobs stated. "However, the best candidate for the position just walked out the door." She sent an accusing glare at Tania.

The petite, well manicured, fashion statement of a woman, glared at Karin, then with her nose in the air spoke. "If she was not able to withstand the inquiries of this Board she certainly will be lacking as a director."

"There were no inquiries, at least not from us," Karin countered. "Only your insults from what I recall."

"Ladies," Devin did not have the time or the inclination to go through a finger-pointing duel between the two women. "The young woman who ran out the door was?"

"To be honest Devin," Tania smiled. "She was so unimpressive I don't recall her name."

"Ruby Lassiter," Cecil spoke as he nodded to Tania.

"Oh yes," she smirked. "Thank you Cecil."

Cecil turned to Devin. "We did not have the opportunity to properly speak with her. However, I found her to be quite straight forward and dead on with her opinions."

"I was impressed with her resume," Devin nodded.

"She was the young woman recommended by the Mayor," Miranda added. "If we did not give her ample opportunity to represent herself, I think it is incumbent upon us to rectify that error. After all, the Mayor will have to be the one to approve the zoning on the facility."

"Well the City Council will have to give its blessing on the proposed site in addition." Tania stated. "As you know, we already have the majority of the votes needed.

"From what I understand," Karin spoke. "Some members of the Council are waiting to hear from the person we select as Director. That conversation may sway their vote."

"All the more reason we should hire someone who represents well and is able to articulate our desires."

"I found her to be quite articulate," Cecil grinned. "She got her point across with the dollar bill."

Karin laughed. "Yes she did. Either way we don't want to keep the City Council waiting if we want this project to begin by the first of the year.

This is the week of Thanksgiving. If we want to speak with them, we need to make a decision today. In two days they will close for the holiday and then we will have to wait until Monday of next week to get started."

"It is my hope to have this project ready to roll by January 1." Devin stated as he sat forward. "Were there any other candidates qualified for the position?"

"Well," Tania spoke quickly. "Jeremy Claiborne is still available. His resume was very impressive."

"I have concerns with him," Cecil sat forward.

"He was the director of a few group homes my company has handled jobs for."

"He dealt with troubled teens for the last five years." Tania looked at the document in front of her as she read off his accomplishments. "He's handled budgets," she looked up, "by the way Ms. Lassiter did not have that on her resume. And he has grant writing skills, which will come in handy in the future."

"But he is asking for a rather hefty salary," Karin cautioned. "There are still unanswered questions regarding incidents at one of the group homes."

Devin listened as he read through both resumes. "What were your concerns with" he looked at the papers in front of him. "Ms. Lassiter?" He looked around the table.

"She was...well untidy, unprepared and frankly rude," Tania replied.

"I think we may have started on the wrong foot with her," Cecil turned to Devin. "I think we should ask the candidate to come back in today if possible."

"I don't think that's a good idea." Tania turned to Devin. "Mr. Claiborne is scheduled to meet with us at one."

"Mr. Upton," Karin spoke. "Ms. Lassiter did not have the opportunity to speak to her qualifications. I have to agree with Mr. Dance. We should ask her to come back today."

"Let's speak with both of them," Devin closed the folder. "Tania please contact Ms. Lassiter to see if she can meet with me this evening."

"Meet with you?"

"Yes. At her convenience." He opened another folder. "Cecil talk to me about this building you've selected for renovations. Give me the cost and timeframe."

Tania opened the next folder perturbed by the outcome of the meeting thus far. It was fortunate that the Lassiter woman came in looking so disheveled. That gave her the ammunition she needed to put Jeremy in that position. If she could get him what he wanted, the better her chance of securing the HR position. She thought it was handled. Now she had to call the woman back in again.

"What are your thoughts Tania?"

"Excuse me?" She'd missed the entire conversation. She had to do better.

"On the location of the facility," Devin explained.

"The location is good," she stated while quickly glancing at the people at the table. When she reached Miranda the woman was staring at her as if she was trying to see through her.

There was something about Tania that never sat well with Miranda. The woman thought as she watched her. She was up to something. Miranda had no idea what, but she would find out. There was a time when Aaron tried to get his new assistant and Devin together. Thank goodness that did not work out. Devin for some reason did not trust Tania and neither did she. Miranda turned her attention back to Devin.

"Then we all agree on the location for Aaron's House," Devin was pleased to announce. "Tania since this is a personal project and not really a task for Upton Investments, I think we should have Cameron as the point of contact for the Director of Aaron's House. I know you are not too fond of this particular project. This will allow you to concentrate directly on Upton."

Cameron Hicks! The name screamed through Tania's mind. That was the other person up for the Human Resources Director position.

"On the contrary, Devin I would like to remain a part of the project."

"Very well," Devin smiled. "We welcome your assistance."

"Now that Devin is the CEO of Upton, I think decorum would call for you to refer to him, at least in public, as Mr. Upton." Miranda smiled. "Don't you agree, dear?"

CHAPTER SIX

Upton Investments was located in downtown Richmond, not far from the Federal Reserve Bank and close to the river. The twenty floor, glass enclosed building was one of the most modern and tastefully decorated in the area. The executive offices were located on the twentieth floor. There were private offices along the outer walls giving those executives' city views or river views. Devin's office, which spanned the width of the building, had both.

At times the view was calming and at others times bustling with activity. Today would be labeled as hectic.

Miranda did not have an official office in the building. However, due to the late hours her husband would pull every so often, he had an office designated for her use only. She hadn't been there much since Aaron's death. But felt these first few months of Devin stepping into the leadership role, her presence would go a long way in smoothing the feathers of some of the men and women who had worked there from the beginning. Some believed they should have been named CEO when Aaron passed away, however, his will stipulated that his son, Devin, would be the lone CEO of the company. That was enough pressure. Miranda did not want anyone to attempt to take advantage of his learning curve, especially someone like Tania.

After the breakfast meeting, they went into the office. Miranda stopped by her office to drop off her purse and umbrella then joined Devin in his office.

"I have no idea how Dad managed to juggle so many things at once." Devon smiled as he pushed papers around that were waiting on the desk when he walked into the office. Mrs. Talley, his secretary, indicated he had twenty messages waiting for him to return calls.

"I placed the more important ones on top. That's the way I did it for you father. If you need me to do it in a different manner, don't hesitate to tell me." The stylish, slim, fifty something woman stated.

"Whatever way you handled it previously will be fine. Please, just let me know when there are urgent matters first thing each morning."

"Very well, Sir." She looked at her tablet. "You have a meeting scheduled with New Account Acquisitions at two and Investment Services at three."

"Thank you Mrs. Talley."

"Oh, Ms. Reid requested I put an interview for a Mr. Claiborne on your schedule at one. Is that acceptable?"

"Yes, I expected that."

"I need you to let me handle your calendar if you plan to get things accomplished." She scowled. "You can't let everyone have access or you will be behind schedule before your day starts."

"Yes Ma'am."

"I'm not scolding, it's just that at times Ms. Reid can be a little pushy."

"No, I have never thought that." Devon looked up and smiled at the woman.

"You have a sense of humor," Mrs. Talley returned the smile." I like that." She turned to see Miranda standing in the doorway." Mr. Upton there is a Mrs. Upton here to see you, shall I show her in?"

Miranda laughed." After all these years you should know when it comes to this office I don't need to be announced." The two women hugged. "How are you this morning Ella?"

"I'm doing well my friend, it is good to see you in the office." Ella turned to Devin. "Will that be all for now Mr. Upton?"

"Yes, thank you Mrs. Talley."

"Now that is the way that you should be addressed," Miranda stated as she stepped into the office and closed the door.

"Oh I think people are just casual around here." Devin removed his suit jacket placing it on the back of his chair. He rolled up his shirt sleeves and took a seat at the desk." Mother, do you happen to know who Dad wanted to head up Human Resources? Did he ever mention a name to you?"

"He did." She replied then took a seat and crossed her legs in front of his desk.

Devin looked up." Will you share that name with me?"

"No for I am certain your father would want you to make those decisions for yourself." She smiled. "I know he had faith in you and so do I. You will make the right decision."

"You're no help," he smiled.

"You so look like your father sitting there," Miranda lowered her head. The mood in the room became solemn. She shook it off. "We are not going there today. Listen, before your next meeting starts, I wanted to speak with you about this morning."

Devin sat back. "Is this another warning about Tania?"

"Yes," she chuckled. "Aaron's House was special to your father. I want to ensure the right person is selected to head it up."

"I know."

"I don't want you to put that selection in Tania's hands. I know how busy you are establishing your ownership of the company. But promise me you will make the selection yourself. Speak with both of the candidates then you determine which will bring your father's dream to fruition."

"Would you like to be a part of that?" He knew what the answer would be before he asked the question but he wanted to put it out there for her anyway.

"I'm not ready, yet." She stood to leave, "But I am getting stronger every day." She walked to the door." I'm going to sort through some more of your father's things and then I'm going to head home. Will I see you for dinner?"

Devin looked at the stacks of paper work on his desk shaking his head. "I'm not sure, I'll give you call."

Miranda opened the door. "I'm calling Dr. Stanton to come in and take a look at that wrist."

Devin held up his hand. "I don't think it's necessary. It's feeling a lot better."

"Okay, son. Dr. Stanton will be in sometime today, I'm sure." With that Miranda Upton was out of the door.

Devin had to smile. He was certain the doctor would be in his office within the hour. He glanced at his desk, turned on his computer and exhaled. "I better get some work done."

CHAPTER SEVEN

Ruby had just walked into her two-bedroom apartment when her cell phone chimed. She placed her wet umbrella in the stand next to the door. Then took the time to hang her coat on the hook by the door to let it dry out before putting it in the closet. She looked up the stairs then decided to go into the kitchen first. It was rare that she had time to herself, especially during the day. Hell, at night her life was hers alone, no other person, man, dog or child. She picked up the teakettle, filled it with water and put it on the stove. Her cell phone chimed indicating a message had been left. Ruby didn't bother to check the caller or the message. She pulled off her shoes and placed them neatly in a corner in the kitchen. Her red leather pumps looked good when she walked out of the house this morning as did, her suit, hair and everything else. But, then the rain, flat tire and the heifer occurred. Ruby smiled as she reached under her skirt to remove her panty hose. "That's a good name for her, Ms. Heifer."

Her telephone chimed again. This time she thought it might be one of her siblings. Ruby was the oldest daughter to eleven brothers and sisters. Six boys who were all named after men in the Bible, Samuel, Joshua, Mathew, Luke, Timothy and Adam, plus five sisters who her father called his precious gems, Pearl, Diamond, Opal, Jade, and Sapphire, who they all called Phire, and had just entered her freshman year of college.

Being the oldest placed the responsibility of helping with the care of the younger children square on her shoulders. From cooking meals, to washing clothes until they were old enough to learn for themselves, to helping with homework, being there to listen about boys from the girls and girls from the boys. To be honest, it all came naturally. Her mother, Sally, would be in the kitchen cooking and Ruby would be right beside her mirroring whatever her mother did. As the babies came, she did the same thing. So as Sally took care of one, Ruby would have the other. When she turned eighteen, she got a job with the city and a year later had her own apartment. She would still go by her parents' when she got off from work. Help with dinner and homework and then would go to her own place. It took a minute to get used to living alone, but as the girls grew older they would spend the night or weekends with her. Her income was okay, but no matter what, when tuition time came around for one of her siblings, she along with her older brothers would pitch in to help their parents. Not one Lassiter under her who wanted to go to college was ever denied the opportunity. Fortunately for her, she was promoted several times at her agency and living from paycheck to paycheck became a thing of the past. She was in no way in the financial shape of her brothers or even some of her younger siblings, but she was okay. She didn't want for much.

Except at night. She did not know it was possible, but she was dealing with empty nest syndrome. With everyone off to college, she found herself with a lot of free time and nothing or no one to fill it with. Oh she still worked forty hours a week and then spent most of her evenings helping at the homeless shelter, but when she came home to her apartment the loneliness would at times consume her. Somewhere along the line, she took a miss step in her life.

"Hello," she answered the call.

"Ruby where should I go to get a really sexy gown for a reasonable price?" Opal, the oldest twin to set number one asked.

"Well, hello. How are you?"

Opal sighed. "I'm sorry Ruby. Hi. Are you busy at work?"

"Hi and no. I'm not at work. I'm home. I have a few discounts on my phone. I'll text them to you. Where are you going?"

"I've been invited to the Mayor's tree lighting ball on Friday. I'm trying to find something to wear."

"That should be nice," Ruby held the phone to her ear with her shoulder as she dropped the ripped stockings into the trash. "Do you have a date?"

"Yes, I'm going with Grant."

"Grant Hutchison, Diamond's friend?" She asked as she climbed the stairs to her bedroom.

"Yes."

"Are you two dating?"

"No, people don't date anymore Ruby. We're just hanging out."

"Oh, excuse me. I'm so old and antiquated. Forgive me."

Opal laughed. "Sorry I didn't mean that. I'm just saying you don't have to be in a relationship with a man to go out with him. You know. You should try it once in a while."

"Between when and when?"

"You could use that excuse before, but you can't now. All of us are out of the house now, including Phire. You have no reason not to date," she said in a teasing tone. Or better yet, let some lucky guy knock through those cobwebs you got growing between your legs."

"Opal it's time for you to get off my phone."

She laughed. "Okay, I'm just saying. It's time for you to get out and live a little. Bye sis."

Ruby disconnected the call and dropped the phone on the bed. "Yeah right. Who wants to date a thirty seven year old, old maid?" Walking to her bathroom door, she stopped in front of the mirror and took a good look at herself. The body was still decent, one hundred thirty pounds, not flabby, flat stomach, and solid thighs. Her hair permed straight, not natural like Pearl's or most people these days, but she wasn't bad to look at, she shrugged her shoulders. "It's been a few years girl." She said to herself as she stripped and jumped in the shower. Time to wash away the cold from the rain, the craziness from grocery shopping for the holidays and all memories of Ms. Heifer.

CHAPTER EIGHT

Tania was holding the phone, waiting patiently, but did not receive an answer. That was fine with her. She left another message. "Ms. Lassiter this is Ms. Reid calling from Upton Investments. Please return this call at your earliest convenience."

"That should satisfy the old bat."

"Which old bat would that be?" Miranda asked from the open doorway.

"Um, well, I was referring to the woman on the phone," Tania lied. "Is there something I can do for you Mrs. Upton?"

"Yes, since you were Aaron's assistant I thought you would know what this was about."

Miranda handed her a sheet of paper with hand written notes.

"Where did you get this?" Tania asked as she read through them.

"It was mixed in with some of Aaron's notes."

Tania nodded as she smiled. "Yes I remember when he came up with this."

"What?"

"Oh, it was an employee incentive idea. He thought it would be fun to grant a deserving employee magic red slippers, you know, like Dorothy from the Wizard of Oz. They would be rewarded the slippers at the Christmas party and granted one wish. The wish could be a trip or anything up to $10,000. They would get to display the slippers in their office until the next year."

"What a wonderful idea," Miranda's eyes lit up. "What ever happened with it?"

Tania shrugged. "It died with him I guess." She saw the moment the light conversation changed.

"Thank you," Miranda replied curtly then walked off.

"What in the hell did I do this time," Tania said to herself.

"It could be the cold way you said it to a woman who is still mourning the loss of her beloved husband," Ella smirked. "There's a Mr. Claiborne here to see you." She stated then walked away.

"Why is everyone so touchy these days," she huffed to herself as she went to meet Jeremy.

Jeremy Claiborne was a delicious caramel color and he knew it. The women on the executive floor drooled the moment he stepped off the elevator. A number of women casually walked by the receptionist desk just to get a closer look.

"Mr. Claiborne," Tania greeted him with a handshake. "It is good to see you."

"Ms. Reid," he nodded.

"Would you follow me," she turned as he watched her from behind.

"You are looking well today."

Looking over her shoulder she asked. "How are the wife and children?"

"Oh, it's like that? No small talk for a brother?"

She walked into the office and closed the door. "We are not supposed to know each other." She rolled her eyes upward. "Did you get a chance to review the questions I sent?"

"I know how to conduct an interview Tania."

"Do you?" she raised an eyebrow. "We have another very strong candidate for the position. I can get you in the door, but you're going to have to do your part."

"I always end up on top," He grinned.

"Jeremy, this is important. Devin is just like his father. He is going make his own decision regarding this position. I might not have a say."

"Listen I can handle the bull with the best. No Ivy League kid will ever get the best of me."

"Your attitude is what concerns me. Devin is not your normal Ivy League grad. He's been around and will detect the bull."

"What? You don't have any faith in me?"

"It's not about faith. It's a $150,000 director's position."

"Are you looking out for me or you?"

Tania sat back in her seat. "Both," she smirked. "You get a position that will afford you the opportunity to continue to get kickbacks on supplies. I get your mouth shut about my past."

He looked around. "I don't see you hurting nowhere. Cut a few corners here and there, we could rack up."

"I'll leave that part up to you. All I want is to move on with my life. Be very clear Jeremy, this is it for me." Tania stood. "Are you ready?"

"I'm always ready."

She frowned over her shoulder. Frustrated she opened the door. "Mr. Upton is anxious to speak with you." She stopped at Ella's desk.

"Mrs. Talley, this is Jeremy Claiborne he has a one o'clock with Mr. Upton."

Ella stood. "If you will have a seat Mr. Claiborne, I will let Mr. Upton know you are here."

"Thank you," Jeremy flashed the megawatt smile her way.

Tania nodded. "Good luck, sir," she turned and walked away.

He was looking around when Ella walked up.

She cleared her throat to get his attention. "Mr. Upton will see you now."

Surprised to see the woman standing so close, he grinned sheepishly as he stood. Ella stepped back and held her hand out for him to go first.

Tania returned to her desk as the telephone rang. "Upton Investments, Human Resources, Ms. Reid speaking."

"Hello, this is Ruby Lassiter. I received several messages from you."

"Yes, Ms. Lassiter. Mr. Upton is requesting a meeting with you this evening at your earliest convenience."

"Why?"

"Excuse me?"

"Why does Mr. Upton want to meet with me?"

"You did apply for a position, did you not?"

"I did and some heifer treated me like garbage. I tend not to associate myself with people who don't know how to treat others."

"You were treated the way you presented yourself. But that is neither here nor there. Mr. Upton would like to see you. How soon can you be here?"

"How about half past never."

"What?"

"You heard me. Look, I have a job. I don't need scraps from you or Upton. To tell you the truth, if you are his representative for Human Resources the man has a warped sense of attracting employees."

"I'm not in the mood for your insults." Tania was appalled by the woman's words, but then remembered, that was exactly what she wanted. "Since you refuse to return to be interviewed. I will share your denial of the position with Mr. Upton. Good day." She hung up the phone and smiled. "Maybe this day can be salvaged after all."

CHAPTER NINE

Jeremy called an hour later. "It's in the bag. I had the man eating out of my hands by the time I walked out." He said.

"I'm happy to hear that, Jeremy. Did he make an offer?"

"Not exactly. He stated he would be in touch by Wednesday. He asked how soon I would be available. I'm telling you. I got this."

They talked a little longer then disconnected the call. Tania waited for a call from Devin or Ella telling her to prepare an employment package for Jeremy. An hour and then two hours had passed and still nothing. She knew she was anxious, but it was now close to four o'clock in the afternoon. She would need time to do the paperwork. She picked up the phone and dialed. "Ella, is Devin in his office?"

"Mr. Upton is in, yes."

What was it with old people and the formalities? "May I have a moment with him?"

The woman did not answer right away. "Ella?"

"I'm checking his schedule. Yes, but only a minute."

Tania huffed. "Control freak."

She knocked on the door and opened it to find Devin hard at work. "You look knee deep," she joked from the doorway.

"I am," Devin waved her in. "Come on in, it's not slowing down anytime soon."

Tania smiled. If she did not have this issue with Jeremy, she could have really had fun with the fine Devin Upton. He was well built, had that chiseled chin thing going on and his father's all-knowing eyes. For thirty-eight, he wasn't a bad looking man. Not at all.

"Devin I was wondering how the interview with Mr. Claiborne went earlier?"

Devin looked up. "It went well. He was very knowledgeable on the business side of a shelter. The budgeting, grants and proposals. Working with the maintenance that would be required," He nodded. "I was impressed."

Tania smiled.

"I still would like to speak with the other candidate for the position. Do you have a time for me to meet with her?"

The smile faded. "I know your mother requested I reach out to the woman, but I still feel we have a strong candidate in Mr. Claiborne and I, for one, would not take the chance on losing him." She shrugged. "Frankly I was thinking you offered him the position before he left."

"I like looking at all my options. Did you reach the woman?"

Tania took a step closer to his desk. "I did and she refused to come back to meet with you."

Devin frowned. "Why would she do that? She did apply for the job, right?"

"Yes, she did."

"What reason did she give for not wanting to come back in?"

"Nothing tangible," Tania feigned indifference.

"Hmm," Devin thought. "Leave her information with me. I'll reach out to her."

Tania panicked, "Devin I don't think a person in your position should beg anyone to interview with us." She shook her head. "Not when we have a viable candidate available."

Devin laughed. "I'm not lowering myself in any way." He picked up his pen and began working again. "This project is important to my family and I want to ensure every step was taken to get the best person for the job." He looked up and smiled. "Leave me the information I'll make the call."

"Yes, Sir."

Devin watched as a dejected Tania walked out of the room. He put the pen down and sighed. Jeremy Claiborne said all the right things, was able to express the right sentiments when it came to business. There was no doubt in his mind that the man would be capable of doing the job. His concern came with whether he would do the job. Devin had worked with men like Jeremy before. They had the knowledge, the skill set and the ability, but they liked to just slide by. They would do enough to say they got the job done, then wait around for someone else to pick up the slack. Devin stood and looked out his window over the city. His dad had picked a good place for his offices. The vast diversity in the community could be seen from his window. Everything from the rundown homes on the east end of the city to the million dollar homes not a block away in a gated community. What Devin was looking for was a person who would care about people whether they lived on the east side or 25th street or the west side. He didn't feel that in Jeremy Claiborne. To top that off, the man asked for a $200,00 annual salary. Devin did not mind paying that if the person was worth it. He just wasn't sure that person was Jeremy Claiborne.

He sat back down at his desk and turned to his computer. Tania had not returned with the information and this was something he wanted off of his plate tonight. He picked up the telephone.

"Ella do you remember the young woman's name who applied for the Aaron's House Director position?"

"Hold on."

He heard her keying into her computer.

"Ruby Lassiter. Would you like her number?"

"Yes, thank you," he wrote the number down on paper.

He hung up then dialed the number.

The call was picked up on the second ring. "What part of I am not coming back to be humiliated again did you not understand? I don't get why you keep calling. You clearly did not want to speak with me earlier today. Was I too shabby looking for your taste? Or was it the dollar bill and you full of crap bit that turned you off? Oh wait, it couldn't have been that because when you asked me to leave I had not said a word to you. Now look, as I told you before. I have a job. It may not be in a fancy office like what you probably have. But I get to touch people's lives in a positive way. Not the way you treated me, but in a way that would uplift and encourage. But I am certain you would have no idea how to do that."

"How would you go about doing that?"

Ruby held the phone away from her ear and looked at the number. She brought it back. "Who is this?"

"Devin Upton."

She closed her eyes and whispered a low curse. "Damn."

"I've had that feeling before. Like I've put my foot in my mouth so how do I take it out without cutting it off?" He nodded. "Yes, I have been in your shoes."

Ruby took a deep breath. "Mr. Upton," she paused. "I am so sorry. I did not mean to say those things to you. I do not know you. And to be honest, I don't think I want to get to know you or your company."

"I think that is a bit unfair since you just about broke my arm earlier today. I would think the least you could do is to sit down and talk with me for a minute to discuss Aaron's House."

Ruby sighed. "I'm very sorry about your arm. Please tell me it's not broken."

Hearing the concern in the woman's voice made Devin feel bad. His arm was sore but certainly not broken. He didn't mean to insinuate that is was. "No, it's not."

He heard the genuine sigh of relief in her voice.

"Please accept my apology for injuring your arm. I was in a hurry to get away from that Ms. Heifer who was handling the interview."

"Who? Never mind. Ms. Lassiter I would like the opportunity to speak with you. Are you free to meet with me? I have no problem coming to you."

There was some hesitation. "Well, I'm due at the shelter by five-thirty. And with the weather threatening to change to snow I suspect we will be busy."

"Where is the shelter located?"

"At the corner of the Boulevard and Cary."

"The Cary Street Shelter?"

"Yes," Ruby nodded.

"I'm not far from there. I could meet you there at five. We could talk for a few minutes and we'll see where it goes from there. Would that work?"

Hesitation again. "I'll see you there at five. How will I know who you are?"

"I'm the one with the broken arm," he teased. She gasped. "I'm joking. See you at five." Devin hung up the telephone and for some strange reason found himself laughing.

CHAPTER TEN

"There are so many children," Devin looked around surprised. The woman at the desk looked up. "The school bus just dropped them off." She smiled. "May I help you with something?"

The children were running around. Some older boys had grabbed a book from one of the smaller children and were throwing it around. A woman walked in from the back and began yelling at the boys. The boys seemed undaunted by the woman and her threats to cut their heads off, for they continued to tease the small boy more.

The book sailed through the air again just as a woman in the best-looking jeans he had ever seen walked by him. The woman who had just walked right past him caught the book in mid-air.

The place, where he couldn't hear himself think a minute ago, was suddenly silent. Not a creature was moving, not even a mouth.

"Ikill, Dollar and Coke, the office, now." The voice wasn't loud or demeaning but the boys moved as if lightening had struck them.

"Yes ma'am," they each replied.

She then walked over to the little boy who was crying. Bending down, she gave the little boy his book said a few words, then waited. The little boy threw himself into her arms. She picked him up and rubbed his back. As the woman turned towards them with the child in her arms, her eyes were closed and she spoke softly. Devin could see this was not an act. She was genuinely concerned for the child.

The little boy had put his head in the crook of her neck and it seemed as if he had no intention of moving anytime soon. The woman embracing the child opened her eyes and smiled.

Devin had a sharp intake of breath. He swore he was looking into the eyes of an angel. Her hair was parted in the middle and hanging to her shoulders. Her skin was the color of a Hershey kiss, and her, lips were "Ruby Red," he wanted to laugh. "Who does that anymore?"

"What?" the woman at the desk asked.

Devin had forgotten the woman was standing there talking to him. "I'm sorry," he turned back to her. "Would you point out Ruby Lassiter?"

"She's right there holding Tyler."

Devin shook his head then turned back to the woman with the child. "Of course she is."

He watched as she directed the other children to an area at the far end of the wide space. She then instructed an older child on how to set up the divider. She took two other older children, placed three younger ones with them and began what appeared to be homework sessions. As she carried Tyler, she approached the woman who had been yelling at the boys earlier. The two started walking towards the front where he stood. Suddenly the place that was in chaos when he arrived was now thriving with constructive activity.

"I'm afraid she may be a minute. Tyler isn't going to let her go for a while. Then Ruby will have to get dinner started and served. I'm afraid she is going to be a little busy until the other volunteer arrives."

"How long has she been working here?"

"Oh, she's not an employee. She's a volunteer here. Lord, Ruby's been doing that since I've been here. And that's been at least five years."

"You've been living here for five years?"

"I don't live here. I'm the Director."

Devin looked at the woman then at Ruby. "You're the Director and she's the volunteer?"

"Yes," the woman nodded.

Something wasn't right with that picture, but it wasn't his place to say anything. Ruby stopped at the desk. "Mrs. Greenwood, may I use your office to speak with the boys?"

"Of course."

"Also, I brought some items for the children. They're in my car. I asked Victoria to get them for me if it's okay with you." She was reaching into her purse, but having a difficult time with the boy still clinging to her. Finally, she hoisted the young boy into his arms. "Tyler go to this nice man."

Devin looked at Tyler and Tyler looked at him. Neither said a word, but Tyler must have decided it was okay for he put his head on Devin's shoulder without making a sound. When seconds ticked by and there was still no sound from the child, Ruby stopped digging for her keys then slowly turned to him. When Devin looked up all three women was staring at him with mouths gaped open.

Ruby finally pulled her keys out of the purse and gave them to Victoria. "Everything should be in the trunk," she said as she reached for the child.

Devin shook his head. "He's fine."

Ruby stared at the man. "Don't tell me. You must be Devin Upton."

He smiled then extended his hand. "Ruby Lassiter."

The man was a reincarnated Joe Lassiter if she ever saw one. Oh he wasn't as tall as her father but he was at least six-three, a solid two hundred pounds, beautiful light brown eyes, and the juiciest lips she had ever seen on a man. Ruby shook the man's hand and was overwhelmed with his strength. Not the strength in a hand shake, but the strength from within. She could feel the confidence in who he was and what he expected out of this life. It was also clear "You are going to make somebody some beautiful babies."

"Mmm hmm," Mrs. Greenwood agreed.

"You can let my hand go now," Ruby smiled. "And I'll take Tyler off your shoulder."

"I think he's asleep," Devin glanced at the boy. "How old is he?"

"Tyler just turned six," Ruby turned. "At least let's go into the office, where you can have a seat and we might get in a quick conversation."

"I'd appreciate that." He followed her into the small office where the three older boys sat waiting.

CHAPTER ELEVEN

They all looked up as Ruby walked in the door.

"Ikill please let Mr. Upton have a seat."

"Ms. Ruby we are sorry for teasing Tyler. It won't happen again," Coke declared. "Ain't that right Dollar?"

"No ma'am it won't happen again I promise."

Ruby looked at each of the boys. "We are our brother's keeper." Their heads rolled upward as each of them stood. They all spoke in unison.

"We are our brother's keeper. We are to never harm but constantly build each other up."

"What does that mean Coke?"

"Aww Ms. Ruby do I have to?"

Ruby simply raised an eyebrow.

"Aww man," the boy sighed. "As the oldest in the center it is my joy to protect, teach and inspire all to be as good if not better than I."

"Did you think for one moment how Tyler felt when you teased him? The person he looks up to the most."

"No ma'am."

"You thought it was a quick laugh to pick on someone smaller than you. You are no longer Tyler's protector."

The boy looked crest fallen. "Ms. Ruby I didn't mean to hurt him."

"That may be true Coke, but you did hurt him." She shrugged "I'm not sure he can trust you to protect him now."

"I'll make it up to him."

She shook her head. "He will Ms. Ruby," Dollar added. "I'll help him."

"What are you going to do differently, Coke?"

"I ain't going to let nobody touch him," the boy proclaimed.

"That's right," Coke added. "If they get through Coke, then they gonna have to go through me next."

"You know my word is my bond, Ms. Ruby," Ikill stepped forward. "Us three," he nodded his head. "We got Lil man. We ain't mean no disrespect, but I can see what you saying, he's little and don't know we was just joking."

"Do I have to turn in my protector's card Ms. Ruby?" Coke asked with his head hanging down.

Ruby looked at each of the boys and sighed. "Let me see your card," she held her hand out.

She wrote the word "temp" on it. "I'm going to let you keep it for a probationary period."

"What dat mean?"

"You have a few days to prove you can protect Tyler," Devin stated then thought about what he did. "Right Ms. Ruby?"

Ruby looked from Devin to Coke. "Right. You have ten days. If you do right by Tyler and the other children you get a new protector's card."

The boys looked at each other excited. "Man you get a new card."

Coke reached out and took Tyler from Devin's shoulder. "When I get my card back I'm gonna help y'all get one too."

"Thank you gentlemen." The boys left the office in reprimand, but in good spirits.

"They are going to bug you until they get a new card," Devin continued to watch the boys.

Ruby watched him and she was still watching him when Victoria walked in with the bags from her car. "It's snowing already?"

"Yes ma'am and it's coming down thick," Victoria said as she gave her the keys. "You want me to start dinner?"

"Yes please. I'll be in the kitchen in a minute," Ruby smiled at the young mother of three.

Victoria looked from the man sitting in the office to Ruby. "I bet y'all would make some pretty babies together."

"Thank you Victoria," Ruby took the keys. "I'll meet you in the kitchen."

"All right, but I'm just saying, damn he's fine."

"Thank you Victoria. Good bye."

Victoria left the office as Ruby closed the door behind her. "I'm sorry for all of that." She sighed as she sat back behind the desk, which was loaded with case files. She stared at him. "How is your arm?"

He held it up showing the black hand brace. "Sprained, not broken."

"I see." She lowered her eyes, and then slowly looked directly at him. "Please forgive me for not looking before I stormed out of the room."

The sincerity in her eyes touched him in a way that made him want to make it all right for her. "Forgiven."

"Thank you," she smiled. "Now, what did you want to speak with me about?"

"Aaron's House," Devin said as he sat forward. "You've been vetted and remain at the top of our list for the Director's position. I came here to interview you for that purpose."

"Mr. Upton..."

"Devin, please."

"Okay, Devin, you seem like a nice enough person. But I have to tell you; the people on your staff aren't too nice. I'm not saying all of them, but that one you have handling your Human Resources department needs some help in the people skills area. I'm a pretty strong woman and she had me thinking twice about my belonging in the same room with her. What would she do with the people around her who are trying to get themselves together? I'm very protective of my people." She pointed out the door. "You see those people coming through that door? They are mine and I will not allow anyone to berate, belittle or be cruel to them in any way. I don't think your organization can say the same."

"I wasn't present at the meeting this morning. I can't speak on what took place. What I can do is ask you to look at our plans for Aaron's House. The programs we have slated to take place are to help the people who are walking through that door. I've watched you for the last thirty minutes turn chaos into structure. I need you to do that for Aaron's House." Devin stood and pulled out a card. He wrote on the back. "This is my offer. Before you say no, come to this address tomorrow around noon. Meet some of the people you will be working with. If you feel the same way, I'll move on to the next candidate. However, if we prove to be worthy, I would like for you to accept the position."

CHAPTER TWELVE

Ruby looked at the card, then flipped it over. "That is a very lucrative offer," her brow creased right in the middle. "You could build a few houses for that amount of money."

"The Upton Foundation is funding this project. We hope to get a few grants to assist in the future.

"Ruby," Mrs. Greenwood walked into the office. "The snow is getting bad. I'm going to leave things in your hands." She grabbed her coat and purse from the bottom drawer of her desk. "I will call in around midnight to check on things."

Ruby smiled. "I'll see you in the morning Mrs. Greenwood. Be safe."

"I will. Call if you need anything."

"Yes ma'am, have a good night."

"Don't tell me, Mrs. Greenwood is the Director here?"

"Yes, she is," Ruby began walking towards the door. "We are going to be getting crowded real soon. You should leave before the storm settles in."

"What about you?"

"Oh, I stay the night to help out with new arrivals."

"How many people are you anticipating?"

"The place can only hold seventy-five," Ruby said as she walked him to the door. She looked at the line that was already forming. "I'm sure we'll get twice that tonight. Most will have to be turned away."

"Ms. Ruby the lady in the kitchen is burning the bread," A little girl yelled.

"I'll be right there."

"How many volunteers do you have?"

"Not enough," Ruby said as the young girl pulled her along.

"Come on Ms. Ruby before she burns the kitchen down."

"Take care of what you need to." Devin waved her off. "I can see myself out." Ruby turned her attention to the situation at hand as she disappeared around the corner.

Adjusting his jacket, he turned to leave, then froze. The line at the door was at least thirty people deep and that was just what he could see. He turned to the desk. There was one person signing people in. Looking out the double glass doors he could see the snow was steady with no sign of letting up. He removed his jacket and walked around the desk.

"Do you have another sign in sheet? We could get two lines going to get them in faster."

"Sure," the woman reached under the clipboard to give him sign in sheets. "The name is Cheryl."

"Devin," he smiled as he pulled out a pen from his pocket. "How much do they need to fill out?"

"As much as possible. Full name is a must. We have to know who is in the building."

Devin nodded. "May I help the next person in line?"

To his dismay, there was a rush of people hurrying towards him.

"A single line, people. You know how this goes," Cheryl turned to him. "You have to be specific when addressing them. Each of them is the next person to the person in front of them." She grinned.

"Sorry," Devin smiled back. Then turned his attention to the line.

An hour later, the line was down to a trickle, but the facility was filled to the brim. He began helping with cots and blankets until an argument broke out about a particular spot in the corner.

"It's my spot. I sleep here near the water cooler every night," the rough looking man with a few missing teeth said. "I want my spot."

"My family was here first," the other man argued as he stood in front of his two little boys and wife. My wife is pregnant and needs to be near the restrooms."

It seemed to Devin the old man was a regular while the younger man and his family were new to the shelter. The children stood behind their mother with fear etched on their faces. Devin saw the younger man trying to stand up for his family. He couldn't stand down. His pride was at stake. Devin looked around for an area for the family. That would be difficult, the place was packed. It would be easier to relocate the man. However, reading people the way he did, he knew the older man would probably cause more trouble than it would be worth.

Someone had alerted Ruby to the situation. She had just walked around the corner to handle Mr. X, that's what he called himself. His name was Ted Hamilton. He was a recluse who had been coming to the shelter as long as Ruby had been there. He could be mean as a rattlesnake and just as deadly to an insecure person. She started to step forward but Devin's words stopped her.

"Sir, thank you for preserving this area. This family could use your help. This is their first time here and we don't know the rules. Could you help us with that?"

"Rule number one, this is my spot. Rule number two I don't like being questioned. Rule number three, I don't do kids."

Devin raised an eyebrow. So he wanted to play it that way. "Okay, I can see you are a straight to the point kind of man. So let me ask you. Did you pay for this spot? Or build it? Or furnish it? When you walked through that door you were given a set of rules to go by. So were they. The number one rule, First come first served. They were here before you. Find another area for tonight. Here is your blanket." Devin held the blanket out for the man. The man stared at Devin as if taking his measure on how far he could go with him. He finally decided to walk away. There was something in the man's eyes that told Devin this was not the end. He looked at the father.

"I'll hang around for a while to make sure he stays away."

"Then what happens tomorrow, or the next day or the next?"

"Let's get your family settled and we'll worry about tomorrow, tomorrow."

To Ruby's surprise Devin took a seat on the floor and sat next to the family and began talking.

"You think he's going to watch over them all night?"

Ruby smiled. "I think he is going to watch Mr. X. All night."

"That's pretty sweet," Cheryl stated.

"Yes, it is," Ruby, acknowledged. "What is his game?"

"Huh, you're his game. During intake, all he did was ask question after question about you." She turned and walked off.

CHAPTER THIRTEEN

Lights were out at ten o'clock and televisions were all turned off by eleven. Ruby had watched him for a while as she checked on the other guests. Now, it was time for her to take a break.

During the night she saw Devin walk outside once. Twenty minutes later he was back with a laptop and a blanket. He retook his seat next to the family, powered up his computer and looked to be working.

It was around midnight, the place had settled down with the exception of one or two people milling about. She walked over with a cup of hot coffee and a container.

"Coffee?"

Devin looked up to see the angel smiling down at him. "Thank you." He took the cup.

"Did you eat anything?"

"I can wait until morning."

Ruby took a seat on the floor next to him. She opened the container of food she had just heated up in the microwave. The aroma hit his nostrils instantly. "I bet you didn't eat lunch, did you?"

Devin thought, then looked sideways at her. "Do you know my mother?"

Ruby smiled. "I don't think so. You just look like the type." She handed him a fork.

"What type is that?" He put the fork into the container and put a forkful of food into his mouth.

"The work at your desk through lunch, dinner and any other meals you can get away with type."

"Hmm, that's good," he dug in again. "What is it?"

"Beef, sausage, potatoes, green and red peppers, onions and a little homemade sauce."

"Someone should patent this and sell it," he dug in again.

"You're not hard to please."

"I love good food."

"I think you are just hungry." She ate. "So tell me, what's your story?"

He stared at her. "What do you mean?"

"You come in here under the pretense to offer me a job. You stay. Help out and now you are acting as guardian angel over this family you don't even know? Why?"

"Are you the only person who can care about people?"

"No," Ruby shrugged as she ate. "But I plan to be here tomorrow. Can you say the same?"

"No," he dug in again. Ruby handed him the container. "I plan to go to work tomorrow. I'm taking Mr. Sanders and his family with me." he smiled. "I'm going to put him to work with a decent salary. Then I'm going to have my mother find them a temporary place to live."

Ruby liked his smile. It was genuine and she knew the intentions in his heart were good. But she had to give him a little reality.

"Then what?" Ruby raised an eyebrow. "What are you going to do when Mr. Sanders' PTSD returns? See, that's how he lost his home and his job. He didn't receive the medical attention he needed to prepare him for his return home from Iraq. So he will have a job and a home. How is he going to keep it?" Devin stared at her. "What are you going to do when Mrs. Sanders loses another child because of his temper? You see Devin money isn't always the answer. Some problems go deeper than what money can fix. In order to help some people you have to teach them to fish in life. That way they can survive once you are no longer a part of their lives. Do you understand?" She sighed. "You are like most people. You think the problem is simple. Throw some money on it. That will fix it." She shook her head. "Look, I know you meant well. The road to hell is paved with good intentions. Take some time. Look deeper before you jump."

Devin was holding the last bite on the fork in mid-air. He wasn't sure why but he just felt like he was slapped. He chewed the last bite as he glanced at the family. It surprised him to see the wife's eyes were staring at him.

"Thank you for the job." She said while lovingly holding the children on one side and rubbing her husband's head with her other hand. "But he's needs help more than a paycheck."

The scene made his heart break. All the time he spent talking with the husband, he was thinking the man had the weight of the world on his shoulders. He was trying to care for a growing family with no job or a roof over their heads. Now he could see the one carrying the burden is the wife. He nodded in understanding. He looked into the office where Ruby had laid on the sofa to relax.

He stood, collecting the container and the fork. "Time to remove foot from mouth."

Standing in the doorway the vision of Ruby Lassiter stretched out stirred more than his intellect. It wasn't just her eyes that were heavenly as he thought earlier. This woman was a total package. Intelligence, beauty and a heart, not to mention the alluring figure his eyes were scanning.

"Don't start something you have no intention of seeing through to the end."

Devin's eyes jumped back up to her face. She was staring at him. Their eyes held. Neither had any thoughts of turning away.

"Are you married? Engaged? Committed?"

"No, no, and no. I'm also too old to play games with someone who is still trying to figure out where they fit in." She sat halfway up and rested her head on her hand as she watched him.

How in the hell did she pick up on that? It was true, he was trying to find his way through being the head person controlling so many lives.

"You are a beautiful woman Ruby Lassiter, inside and out." That was unexpected. Ruby flinched at his words. Devin raised an eyebrow. "I can't imagine you have never been told that."

"My father tells me that all the time."

"I'm not your father. I'm a man who appreciates beautiful things."

"You are also a man who has offered me a job. Which means you may be my boss in a few days."

He nodded. "Professional conflict." He thought for a moment. "Adversity is one of the most powerful motivators known to man. It has a way of making the most ordinary person do the most incredible things. It makes a man try harder for the things he wants. It's one of the reasons why I never give up on possibilities."

"Are you talking about you and me or the Sanders?"

He gave her a crooked smile. "Both."

Ruby liked looking at him. Even in the semi-darkness of the shelter he was a very nice specimen of a man. It was at that moment she felt a tingle between her legs. Cobwebs are awakening she thought to herself. She sat up in an attempt to keep herself from laughing out loud. "Whew," she shook her head. Trying to get her mind off the body's natural reaction to a fine man in a dark area. She glanced at him then frowned. "Where's your laptop?"

CHAPTER FOURTEEN

"Is that code for I'm not interested?"

Ruby stood laughing. "No. It's just a question."

"I left it in the area where I was sitting."

Ruby started walking out the office door. "Lord rescue me from naive people."

"Naive?" He followed her to his spot.

She looked around, moved the blanket then turned to him. "Where did you leave it," she whispered, already knowing the answer.

"Right th..." he stopped then looked around. "I know I left it here."

Ruby held out her hand. "Your phone."

"You're not calling the police." He held it out but did not release it."

"No," she took the phone. "Your code?" He touched the screen with his finger. "You do have the location app on here, right."

"I do," he continued to look around.

"Is your computer registered?"

"Of course," the response was a little clipped.

"Shh, we don't want to wake anyone." Ruby stated as she played with the app. "We simply want to locate your computer."

"I'm sorry. I'm frustrated with myself for not thinking."

"Well, it's here," Ruby looked around. She saw a movement out of the corner of her eye. Of course it was him, she wanted to smack herself. Instead, she turned back not realizing how close Devin was behind her. Their bodies bumped causing her to lose her balance. His arm circled her waist to keep her from falling.

"Whoa," he held her close. "I have you." He smiled down at her as he adjusted their bodies. "Do you feel that fit?"

Did she feel it? Hell yeah, she felt all of him right at the juncture with the melting cobwebs. The contact had Ruby's body tingling like it hadn't for a long...long...long time.

"Foul, foul on the play Mr. Upton." She stepped away. "Now." She took a moment to gather her senses. "I believe I can locate your device."

"Did you?" he gazed into her eyes."

Ruby swallowed. "Yes," she stared at his lips. Why hadn't she noticed how thick and smooth they were before. She pushed away. What was she doing out in the open about to maul a man. "Your computer," she walked past him then stopped where she saw the movement a moment ago.

"Mr. X."

The old man wrapped his blanket tighter around him turning his back to her. Devin started to grab the blanket, but Ruby's hand on his shoulder stopped him. She shook her head.

"He took what's mine, I take what's his." The old man huffed.

Ruby glanced at Devin then sighed as she bent down to the man. "Mr. X. It's Ruby. Now I know you can't see too well, but you can certainly hear me. I realize someone is in your spot tonight. You had to adjust to feeling your way from this new area. But you did it. I watched you all night and you did great. If you think about it, in a way the family helped you to grow. You can expand your choices now. That's a good thing...right?"

How big is this woman's heart? Devin thought to himself. He could feel her empathy towards the man and his situation. He could kick himself for not looking deeper as she said earlier. He had no idea the man had difficulty seeing.

"You gonna send me away?"

"If you want to stay, you have to apologize to Mr. Upton." She heard the man groan and smiled. "I tell you what. If you do it I'll give you a hug."

With a speed Devin did not anticipate, the man threw the blanket aside. He stood and turned to Devin.

"I sincerely apologize for securing your computer." Mr. X held the computer out.

It was now clear the man could not see where he was standing. He took the computer. "Thanks for securing it for me."

Mr. X held his arms out and Ruby walked right into his arms. Her hug was sincere as was Mr. X. The man settled back down and Devin could have sworn there was a smile on his face.

"I want to look deeper," Devin said as they walked back to the office.

Ruby yawned. "It takes time."

He leaned against the doorframe. "I'm not talking about the people."

She turned and glared at him. "It takes time for that too."

He glanced at his watch. "I have time. Let's take a walk in the snow."

"It's almost two in the morning."

"Then no one should be on the road," he smiled.

"It's not the kind of neighborhood you just stroll in."

He took her coat off the rack and held it out. "I'll protect you."

"A man with confidence. I like that," she replied as she slipped her arms into the coat.

The snow was still coming, now blanketing the area. The light from the lamppost glistened over the crystals, making a usually worn area sparkle.

"I love the snow," Ruby smiled as she pulled her hood over her head and stepped out.

"Why is that?" Devin asked as he pulled his gloves from his trench coat pocket. Once they were on, he moved to the outside of the sidewalk area as they walked.

Looking at the sky, she smiled then looked at him. "Something about leaving your footprints as you walk. Look behind you, those are your prints. You made a mark somewhere." She looked forward. "You can't do that in the rain. You can only see your existence in the snow."

"From what I've seen in the last eight hours you leave a print of your existence on a number of people."

"The people in the shelter only see a friendly face that changes into another when they move on."

"I think you are selling yourself short. It's hard to forget the face of a person who shows you kindness. Or someone who has touched your heart."

"Ha, I haven't touched a person's heart in a long time."

Devin stepped in front of her and began walking backwards. "Are you referring to a man or people in general?" he smiled.

"You have a rather disarming smile, Mr. Upton."

He stopped. "Devin," he held her eyes. "We had a moment inside the shelter."

Ruby inhaled. "We did."

"I've been known to let moments pass me by when I was younger. I'm now thirty-eight years old. There aren't too many more moments out there." He stepped closer to her and smiled when she did not step back. "You stepped away before."

"Eyes were upon us."

He nodded. "Is that the only reason?" He tilted his head. "There isn't someone your heart is longing for, your body yearns for, that I should know about?"

The intensity in his eyes had her speechless. All Ruby could do was shake her head no.

"Good," he lowered his head to hers. "Have you ever been kissed Ruby Lassiter?"

"Yes," surges of longing coursed through her from his closeness.

"I don't think you have been, not like this." Their lips gently touched with that first sweet kiss. Then they parted allowing their tongues to touch. Devin wrapped his arms around Ruby's waist, bringing her body snug to his. The blood in his veins awakened with an excitement he had not experienced in a long time. The heat from the kiss warmed their bodies as the falling snow simply melted as it touched them.

Delicious was the only word Ruby could bring to mind. The moment their tongues touched, she knew this was what she had been waiting for all her life. This moment when the fluids in her body began to come ablaze with wanting, longing to be released. The exuberance of finally being kissed to the very core of her soul urged her to move closer, to go deeper exploring all the recesses of his mouth.

Her arms circling his neck quickened the pace of the kiss to a point where he knew he had to stop. His tongue slowly retracted, as he left sweet kisses upon her lips. "You are indeed a precious gem, Ruby Lassiter," he whispered against her lips.

They stood there, in the snow at two something in the morning in a part of town where most people would not walk in the light of day, kissing, and Ruby had no desire to move. "My father says the same thing." She smiled, then lowered her head.

Devin used a finger under her chin to bring her eyes back up to his. "He must be a very insightful man." He pulled her arms from around his neck, then held her hand. "I'm taking you back inside before I strip you down to nothing and make love to you in the snow."

Ruby raised an eyebrow. "I have a feeling we would melt a lot of snow in a short period of time."

"That was hot," Devin closed his eyes.

Ruby shrugged. "You got to the fifty yard line."

Really? Only the fifty? Hmmm." "I think you just left your foot prints back there."

Ruby looked behind them. "I see two sets of foot prints."

Devin stopped and looked back. Devin looked over the area with the snow falling in a new light. "I think I like the idea of your footsteps being next to mine." His eyes met hers.

She wanted to kiss him again, but they had reached the door. "You need to go home Mr. Upton."

"You kiss me and get me all stirred up then send me home." He kissed her gently on the lips. "You're a tease Ruby."

"You have no idea what's going on inside my jeans right now. Let's just say you are not the only one with something stirring."

Devin laughed. "I'm happy to hear that."

"Come inside and get your things."

"You promise to come tomorrow?"

They gazed at each other and laughed again. Ruby blushed. "That will be totally up to you Mr. Upton."

As Devin drove home the woman known as Ruby Lassiter filled his mind. He could not resist thinking about the many things he learned from her while at the shelter. But it was the kiss that not only filled his mind but continued to throw his body into a tailspin. Where in the hell had she been all his life? Moot point. She was here now and he had no intention of letting her go.

The people in the shelter concerned him. Ruby was right, money was needed, but a plan on how to identify and provide services to the individual families selected, was just as important. To think his father once lived that way, consumed him. If he could get out, others could do the same. The need was infinite. After tonight he believed he and Ruby could help. Yes, Ruby Lassiter was the woman for the job and for him.

CHAPTER FIFTEEN

Sleep never found its way to Ruby. So by six a.m. she was ready to turn over the reins of the shelter to the next shift. On the way home, thoughts of Devin consumed her. Who was he? She knew his name of course, but what was he about? Where had he been all her life? Did God send him to tempt her or was he the real thing? "Stop asking questions Ruby. Just...enjoy the moment. Don't read too much into it." She exhaled. With five sisters you would think there was someone she could talk to about this stuff. But her sisters always came to her for advice. They may not feel comfortable doing that anymore if she went to them with her problems.

As she pulled up into her cleared driveway she saw her father shoveling the snow from the sidewalk. He is going to work himself into an early grave, she thought as she shook her head. "Morning Dad," She kissed his cheek. "The sun isn't even up and you are out here working."

"Hey baby girl," Joe kissed her cheek. "I thought I would be finished before you got home."

Ruby took the shovel. "You gave me a nice strong back and taught me how to take care of my lawn. You need to go home to Sally and get some rest yourself." She eased the rebuff with a smile. "After you have a cup of coffee with me, that is."

Joe had removed his coat and gloves, then wrapped his hands around the hot cup Ruby sat in front of him. "You're not going into the office today?"

Ruby finished pouring herself a cup then took a seat. "I've been asked to come back in for a second interview with a non-profit."

"Congratulations baby," Joe smiled. "That must mean they are really interested."

"I think they are, it's just that..." she cleared her throat. "The man heading up the project came by the shelter last night."

When she did not say more Joe spoke. "To see you in action, I take it."

"Kind of. Any way we had a.... moment," she looked at her father to see if he caught on.

"Mmm, hmm. Did this moment involve a kiss?"

"Yes," she replied quickly, relieved he got it.

Joe smiled. "Was it a good kiss?"

"Daddy," she stretched out across the table shaking her head. "I don't even know the words to describe how good it was."

Joe sat back. "That good, huh?"

She sat up. "That good."

"Is this your first time meeting the man?"

"Meeting him, yes, but not the first time I saw him. Anyway if I take the job any chance at us exploring what we discovered last night will be out of the question."

"Why? You are a woman and he is a man. The job is just titles." He stood and put on his coat. "It doesn't change what a man feels when he meets a woman. I don't care who's the boss." He kissed her on the cheek. "A kiss is the most intimate action that can happen between two people. Think about it. How do you turn sex into lovemaking? It's all in the kiss." He raised an eyebrow. "I'll tell your mother you said hi." He smiled and walked out of the door.

Rudy sat at the table for a long time after her father left. He was right, of course. She had had sex before and it felt nowhere near as passionate as the kiss she shared with Devin. Ruby looked at her watch. It was close to eight. She could make it to work by nine if she got up right now, took her shower and headed out. Yep, she could do that. Instead she picked up the phone and called in. She would take a nap then go check out Aaron's House.

This time Ruby wasn't going to try to impress anyone. After all, they were now imposing on her time. At least, when she started dressing, that's what she told herself. Ten outfits later, she decided to wear her sexy power suit. The one she wore when meeting with men who could help with things at the shelter, a navy blazer and skirt that showed off her thick thighs in a flattering way. A pair of three inch black pumps that enhanced her calves and a sexy white crepe blouse that she thought covered her breasts. After all, there was no way she could ignore the six-figure offer or the man who delivered it. By the time she reached Aaron's House, she was soaked from melted snow that was splashed over her stockings and caramel coat. She had slipped several times in the heels and the wind had blown her hair that she took twenty minutes curling.

The building surprised her. It looked like every other condominium building in downtown Richmond. Maybe better than some she had seen. Walking into the lobby, the receptionist greeted her.

"Hello, may I help you?"

She asked the question with a smile even though Ruby looked a mess. "I'm sure you won't believe this but I'm supposed to meet someone here about a job."

"Are you Ms. Lassiter?"

"I am."

The woman came from behind the desk. "Oh, you had an accident. May I take your coat? Would you like something hot to drink?"

"That would be wonderful." Ruby brushed her hair down as the woman took her coat.

"I'm Cameron Hicks," she said as she hung the coat up in a closet. "I wasn't expecting you until noon." The woman shook her hand. "Welcome to Aaron's House."

"Thank you," Ruby slipped out of her heels. "I apologize for my appearance. The snowfall from last night hasn't been kind to me."

"Oh don't worry about it. I have some slippers under my desk. You are welcome to them." Cameron pulled them out and Ruby happily accepted them.

"Red slippers," Ruby smiled. "Thank you."

"You're welcome," Cameron smiled. "Mr. Upton isn't due until noon. I'd be happy to show you around."

Ruby glanced at her watch. She was an hour early. Oh well. Maybe she was more anxious than she thought. "I'm a little early."

"It's not a problem," Cameron held her hand out. "Let's start with the model apartment. Then I will show you the facility."

"Sounds good." Ruby inhaled as she walked behind the slim stylishly dressed woman. Slim, she said that already. Was everyone woman around Devin gorgeous? Walking inside the model apartment took all thoughts of how beautiful the woman was from her mind. There was a living room, a family room and a kitchen with beautiful appliances. Between the two bedrooms on one side of the condo, were a Jack and Jill bathroom and on the other side was a nice size master suite with an on-suite bath, and walk in closets. There was a balcony and a small yard for the children to play.

"It feels like a home," Ruby said as she looked around. It didn't feel like temporary living quarters. It felt like a great place to get a new start.

"That's what Mr. Upton was going for. He wanted the places to feel like a home. "Construction is still in progress on the upper levels but I can show you the medical and entertainment centers."

Cameron was a sweetheart. Ruby recognized her people skills as they toured the complex. She was the type of person that would help and not judge. Twenty minutes later they had returned to the first level when Cameron opened a door. "This will be your office."

Ruby started to say she hadn't taken the job, but then she walked into the office and froze. Devin was there, sitting behind the desk, dressed as if he was meeting the President or somebody. She would have looked good too, if it hadn't been for the mishaps on the way.

The moment Ruby walked into the office Devin laughed. He loved the spirit of the woman and had not even said hello before looking her up and down. "Trying to prove a point."

Ruby looked at her attire and joined him. "Honestly I know how to dress for an interview. It must be you." Ruby declared. "But hey, I am who I am. You accept me or reject me, but clothes are not going to change who Ruby Marie Lassiter is on the inside."

"That makes me a very fortunate man. I happen to like Ruby Marie Lassiter, red slippers and all."

Cameron walked out of the office smiling as she closed the door behind her.

CHAPTER SIXTEEN

"Well, what do you think of the complex?"
"It's wonderful, but how do you decide who's worthy and who is not?"

Devin stood, leaving the chair behind the desk vacant. "I don't." He held his hand out to the chair. "You do." Devin wasn't one hundred percent convinced she would take the position. To ensure the outcome he wanted Devin added. "Before you make a decision, you should know the Director of Aaron's House reports to the Board of Directors of The Upton Foundation, not me personally. As of this morning, I removed myself as the head of the Board and asked my mother to take over." He walked towards her. "I explained that I met an incredible woman who made me feel things I've never felt before." He stopped in front of her and whispered. "I told her the sweetest Ruby red lips I've ever tasted were on that woman and I would not be able to resist kissing them again."

He captured her lips and the sensations from the night before flooded through Ruby. The small amount of cobwebs left from the kiss the night before dissipated as juices began to flow through her panties. The man could kiss her into an orgasm.

"Excuse me," an appalled Tania screeched from the doorway.

"I tried to stop her Mr. Upton," Cameron explained.

"If she had, she would not have been doing her job," Tania made a note to fire Cameron as soon as she was named HR Director. "Ms. Lassiter. I need a moment with Mr. Upton."

"No," Devin turned to Tania. "She stays."

"Devin...Mr. Upton as the Acting-Director for Human Resources it's my job to protect the company from sexual harassment claims." She all but rolled her eyes at Ruby. "This," she turned back to Devin, "is dangerous territory, sir."

He knew she was right and it was her job to point out a cautionary warning. "You are correct Tania," Devin glanced at Ruby. "However, Ruby has not accepted the position and I am no longer in charge of the Foundation. Technically we are on good standing."

"Technically, that may work. But it's the appearance of this, whatever it is that will not be good for the company."

"It's a moot point Tania, the decision has been made."

Cameron knocked, then walked into the office. "Mr. Upton, Mr. Dance would like to see you upstairs."

"Please tell him I'll be right there Cameron, thank you." He turned to Ruby. "I'll be right back," he then walked towards the door as he spoke. "Tania, please ensure all documents are provided to Ms. Lassiter should she decide to stay," he smiled at Ruby then walked out of the door.

"Well, you work fast," Tania turned on Ruby. "In less than twenty four hours, you've worked your way to sleeping with the boss."

"Sounds like you're a little jealous to me. What, you weren't able to get him into your bed?"

"I don't have to," Tania smirked. "I have a Masters in Human Resources Management. A degree, sweetie, something you don't have. I fit in his world. You barely graduated from high school. Speaking of which, how long do you think you will be able to keep his interest?" She looked Ruby up and down. "I mean look at you." She walked around Ruby. "Is the mud and red slippers a new trend or something? What are you going to do when he has business dinners to attend? Or when he is invited to the Governor's Mansion for the holidays? How will you be able to support and represent him if you don't have the education or the fashion sense to be in the same room with his colleagues? You know there is nothing wrong with having hopes and dreams. Your dreams should stay on the level of possibilities. Devin is not one."

"What is it with you? From the moment you put eyes on me it's been a beat a sista down thing with you. Why is that? Do I remind you of somebody who used to beat your ass in high school or something?" Ruby held up her hand.

"Don't answer that, 'cause I really don't care."
She took a step closer to Tania and grinned. "I
think it befuddles you that you have all the
things you mentioned and a man like Devin still
doesn't want you. You ever think it might be
your personality." Ruby turned, walking
towards the door. "Loosen up, get wet," she
looked back over her shoulder. "Don't be afraid
of a little mud." Ruby laughed and opened the
door. "Get the paper work ready. I'm taking the
job." She closed the door behind her.

Tania cursed under her breath, then made a
call. "She's taking the job."

"I thought you had this in the bag?"

"Well, I don't," she huffed. "Give me thirty
days. I'll have her out."

"Yeah well, you better do something. I think
they are picking up on my little business at this
facility and I'm going to need a new gig."

"What's happening?"

"One of the assistants is checking the
supplies as they come in. She came to me about
shortages. I told her some things are on back
order."

Tania shrugged. "Send me a list. I'll see what
I can get to you." She disconnected the call. She
took a seat behind the desk then opened her
briefcase. Using her tablet she pulled up the
paper work needed to officially hire Ruby
Lassiter.

"Why are you sitting behind that desk?"

Tania glanced up to see Miranda standing in
the doorway. She looked back down. "I'm doing

as your son requested. Preparing the paperwork to hire that horrid woman."

"Cameron can take care of that," Miranda walked in and placed her purse on the table near the door. As she removed her coat, she continued. "I would prefer that you stay away from this building."

"Mrs. Upton, it is not my intent to be disrespectful," she looked up. "I answer to your son. He requested I handle this and that's what I plan to do." Tania looked back at her tablet as if dismissing the woman.

Miranda took the tablet from her hand. "You answer to him at Upton, not at Aaron's House." She held her hand out with Tania's coat. "You also do not handle Aaron's House employees. I think you know your way out."

Tania stared at Miranda. "What is it you don't like about me? I worked hard for your husband. I am just as dedicated to your son. I don't understand Mrs. Upton."

"The simple fact that you think it's okay to speak to me with that superior attitude of yours. You didn't work hard for Aaron. You used other people to make you look good. Devin isn't easy to fool. He'll figure out your game, whatever it is. You thankfully are not my problem to figure out." She held the woman's coat open.

Tania grabbed the coat as she walked into the lobby. Devin and Ruby were standing near the elevator talking. They were getting too cozy too quick in her opinion. She walked over and placed her hand on Devin's arm handing him her coat.

"I'm going back to the office," she said sliding into the coat, spreading her hair over the collar. "We still on for dinner?"

"Yes, at seven."

Tania smiled. "I look forward to it." She nodded. "Ms. Lassiter congratulations." She turned and walked out the door with her head held high.

"Dinner?" Ruby raised an eyebrow.

Devin smiled. "Is that a little bit of jealousy I hear?"

Ruby glared at him. "Is there a reason for me to be jealous?"

"It's a business dinner."

"Mmm hmm," Ruby replied. "I can tell you what you can do with your business dinner," she started to walk off.

"Wait," Devin grabbed her hand before she could get too far. "Does this mean you're not taking the job?"

"Oh no," Ruby turned to him. "I'm taking the job. I'm just not sure about the man."

"There you are," Miranda walked towards Devin then stopped. "It is you," she smiled brightly as the woman turned. "Devin this is the woman who helped me the other day with my car."

"Hi," Ruby took the woman's hand. "It's nice to see you again. Thank goodness you didn't have a flat today."

'You're right,"

"Flat? What flat?"

"Oh," Miranda waved his question off. "The day of the Board meeting I had a flat tire and this is the woman who helped me. By the way, I'm Miranda Upton, Devin's mother."

Ruby was surprised. "Ruby Lassiter. It is nice to officially meet you."

Miranda took Ruby's hand and walked away. "Same here. Please tell me you are accepting the position here at Aaron's House. It's a wonderful facility and needs someone who cares to bring it to life."

Devin watched as they walked away talking as if they were life long friends. She changes flat tires. He thought, yet another side to Ruby Lassiter. He liked it. He liked it a lot.

Cameron looked up at him. "And yet another one bites the dust," she smiled.

"You like her?" Devin asked.

"I do," Cameron replied. "She asked the right questions. Voiced the right concerns. You picked a good one Mr. Upton."

"I think I'll keep her." Devin smiled then walked into the office with the women.

CHAPTER SEVENTEEN

It was Thursday morning, Thanksgiving Day and she was in a funk. After officially accepting the position the day before, Ruby and Miranda spent hours going over plans for Aaron's House. Precisely at six-thirty Devin stood to leave.

"Where are you going?" Miranda asked.

"To have dinner with the heifer known as Tania," Ruby huffed.

Miranda laughed so hard it even made Devin smile.

"Mother, don't encourage her."

"That's exactly what I'm going to do." She laughed. "It's about time someone got the balls to stand up to that heifer." She continued laughing.

Devin put on his coat to leave. "I can see now I'm going to have to chaperone you two." He held Ruby's eyes. "May I see you later?"

"You mean after you have dinner and lord only knows what else, with the heifer. No, I don't think so."

Ruby sat in her car outside her parent's home and took a breather. The words from Tania weren't far off the mark. She didn't have the opportunity to attend college like her younger brothers and sister. But she made a good living for herself. After talking to Miranda, she got a glimpse into their private lives. While she and Devin both lived conservatively, they were wealthy. The people in their circle were the elite of the Richmond area and surrounding counties. It wasn't her kind of world. "Tania may be a heifer and I don't have to like her, but she spoke the truth.

Ruby took a moment to pull herself together. She knew once she entered, there would be non-stop activity from cooking dinner to the annual football game, and finally sitting down at the table with the people she loved most in the world.

Ruby walked through the kitchen door to find her parents in a conference with two of her brothers, Joshua, who was always in trouble and her youngest brother Adam who was following in his footsteps.

"I am so happy to see you," Sally beamed as she reached for her.

Ruby hugged her mother, "Hi Mom." She said then looked at her two brothers. "What have you done?"

Adam took a step closer to Joshua, who sat up straight.

"Nothing," the two men replied in childlike voices.

"That sounds like an untruth if I ever heard one," Ruby said as she pulled off her gloves and coat and put them on the hook by the door. She saw Adam's coat thrown across a chair at the kitchen table. She rolled her eyes at him as she picked it up and hung it up. "Did the hook move?"

"No," Adam replied. "I wasn't thinking when..."

"That's just it," she walked over to the sink to wash her hands. "Men don't think," she huffed. "No, they do think, but they think with their dicks instead of their heads."

Sally's eyes grew in size as Adam spoke. "Aren't they one and the same?"

Ruby slowly turned from the sink glaring at him as did Sally.

Joshua stood. "That's my cue to leave." He walked out of the room.

Adam stood there a moment longer. "I...I think, I'll join the guys."

"You do that," Sally sighed, then looked at Joe. "Ruby," she gently rubbed her shoulder. "I'm going to check on the kids then I will be right back so we can talk." She gave Joe a talk to your daughter look, then left the room.

Ruby turned back to the sink. She watched as her father moved from the table, then stood. She knew he was waiting for her. She turned and walked right into his embrace. He rested his chin on the top of her head and held her tight.

"Daddy why do men have to be so stupid?"

"Because we think with our lower extremities rather than with our heart."

Ruby laughed. Joe rubbed her back, happy to see her smiling. He held her at arm's length. "You want to talk about it?"

She stepped back and sighed. "You and mom raised me right. I'm a good person. Why can't men see that?"

"Men or a particular man?" Joe leaned against the counter as Ruby began to do what she does...take care of people. He listened as she checked the greens that were sitting on the stove. She turned them back on, then checked the turkey that was cooking in the oven. Then she picked up the bowl of potatoes and began preparing that. Yes, she was his first baby girl. In his eyes, she was beautiful, all his girls were. But Ruby, well she had a special place in his heart.

As he listened, it became clear to him that Ruby's problem wasn't the man. It was the people around him. "Does he have any idea you have feelings for him?"

Ruby finally stopped. During the entire time she was talking, she had been going from one dish to the next never skipping a beat in the conversation or the meal preparation.

"Oh, no Daddy," she looked up as she placed the now completed potato salad into the refrigerator. "He's my boss for one and for two the man is just...way to fine for someone like me. Now, Opal or Jade," she nodded. "They would catch his eyes."

"Why your sisters? You are just as beautiful as they are."

"Yeah, Daddy, to you. But men like him, they look at the young, slim women with everything in the right place."

Joe smiled. He knew better than to get into the topic. "If this man is worth his weight in gold as you say he is, he will see through all the outside glam and see your heart."

Ruby stared at him. "When did you start using words like glam?"

He glanced up. "Phire," they both laughed at the same time.

Her mother, who had been standing in the doorway listening walked back in. "This has certainly been a busy kitchen today. "Joe, the boys are ready to set up the football game."

"I'll join them," as he walked by, he squeezed Ruby's hand.

Sally put the apron around her waist. "I heard what you said to your father about Opal and Jade." She opened the oven and checked on the turkey. "All of my daughters are beautiful, inside and out. Look at you. You have that Janet Jackson, during the Nutty Professor 2, thing going on. Now that girl, she looks good during Rhythm Nation and Love Will Never Do Without You."

"Hey, Love will never do without you," Opal sang as she walked into the kitchen.

"Work it out somehow," Jade walked in dancing and soon all the women began singing.

Jade the dancer began doing the moves. "They said it wouldn't last."

The back door flew open and in walked her baby sister Phire. "Ohhhh, Love will never do, never do without you." She jumped in. Soon the kitchen was in full Thanksgiving mode as thoughts of Devin moved to the back of Ruby's mind.

CHAPTER EIGHTEEN

Something was missing. It was the first time in Ruby's life that she felt that way at Thanksgiving dinner with her family. Everyone was home, Samuel, Cynthia and their children. Joshua and Roc, with Teddi who had to be a Lassiter, but she didn't ask any questions. Pearl and Theo announced they were having a baby. Luke, Mathew, Timothy, Opal and Jade were there arguing over the loss of the game to the women...again. Opal and Jade teased them unmercifully. But now they were all preparing to go dancing. The surprise of the night was from Adam her baby brother who brought a woman home for Thanksgiving. If that wasn't bad enough, Phire spent the evening talking about some boy from school. It seemed her younger brothers and sisters were moving on with their lives, yet she was stagnant. It seems she was still stuck in the same place. In the kitchen cleaning up, preparing plates for people to take home then putting the food away.

"Hey Ruby," Opal peeked into the kitchen. "We're going to the club. You want to go?"

Ruby looked over her shoulder as she washed the dishes. "No, you go. Have fun."

"Okay, you should drop by later."

"We'll see," she knew when she said it; the club was not in the plans for her. What did she look like going to the club with them? She was too old.

"Ruby," Cynthia called out. "Joe and Sally are keeping the grands. Samuel and I have are going to catch a movie, you want to go?"

Now they wanted her to be a third wheel. "No, thank you. Have a good time." She smiled and continued with the cleanup.

Sally walked in the kitchen as Joshua and Roc carried Teddi to the car. "She is an adorable little girl." She smiled while waving goodbye.

"An adorable little princess," Ruby replied.

The tone of her voice must have been sad, for her mother turned and stared at her. Ruby raised an eyebrow. "What?"

"Why are you hiding out in the kitchen?"

"I'm not hiding out. I'm cleaning up."

"Grown people live in this house. They don't need you to clean up behind them."

"How well I know."

"Ruby?" Sally touched her arm. "What's going on?"

"Nothing...Mom," she shook her head then looked around. "Everything has been put away. So you should be good for the night." Ruby kissed her mother's cheek. "I'm going to the shelter to see if they need me there."

"Ruby, we need you. We will always need you."

Looking into the family room where Pearl and Theo sat, her feet in his lap. "They're happy," Ruby gave a faint smile. "I missed out. Somewhere along the line I missed the dating, falling in love."

"I don't think you missed it at all Ruby," Sally hugged her. "You have always been the one staying home and helping with one thing or another while your brothers and sisters were out enjoying themselves. Now that they are grown, you feel like they don't need you anymore. Well, they still do. But I think it's time for you to live for you."

Ruby walked out of her mother's embrace. "After you've lived a certain way for thirty years it's hard to change." She took her coat off the hook. "I'll see you later."

Climbing into her car, Ruby thought about what her mother had said. Live for me. How do you do that at thirty-seven? Ruby started the car and drove to the shelter. It hadn't snowed today, but it was still cold outside. She wasn't scheduled to be at the shelter. Thanksgiving was always family day at the Lassiters, so she never volunteered. It wasn't like she had anything else to do. Oh, she knew she could have gone out with everyone too. But why, when fifteen minutes in she would begin to feel out of place. Ruby parked her car. That's what she felt. For the first time in her life, she didn't know what her purpose was anymore. She turned off the motor and sat there for a while thinking. The new position would take up a lot of her time and that was good. It came at a good time. First thing

Monday morning, she would give her job a two-week notice of her departure. For now, she would get a head start on selecting families from the files at the shelter. She nodded. "Okay, that's a start." She stepped out of the car and almost screamed.

Swinging her purse, she yelled. "Don't scare me like that."

"Ouch," Devin grabbed the purse and the arm attached to it. "What in the hell do you have in that thing?"

Ruby removed her arm from his grasp. "Something to knock out men who lie. Mr. I'll call you after dinner."

"I called you several times," Devin glowered. "Why aren't you answering my calls?"

Ruby stepped back. He was angry. Not one to mince words, she pulled out her cell phone, put the password in then held it out to him. "Show me."

Knowing he called several times, Devin had no problem taking her phone. He checked the call log and was surprised to see there was nothing from his number. He returned her phone then pulled out his. He gave it to her. "Aaron is the password."

Ruby thought for a moment. Men didn't give women their phones much less the password. She took the phone and saw where he had dialed a number similar to hers but it was off by one digit. "This is not the number I put in your phone." She corrected the number, then gave it back to him.

"When you did not answer I went to the address on your application. Sat outside your condo for hours. You never appeared. I figured this would be my best bet."

Hmm, Ruby thought. He is a little beyond mad.

"When we kissed I felt my world tilt. Women who can kiss are a dime a dozen. The woman who can turn your world upside down is the one you keep." He took a step closer to her. "I did not play games with women when I was young and I am certainly not going to start now. I've had five women in my life. One in high school, one in college and one while I was in Boston. My mother is number four and you are number five. I did not play games with women when I was young and I am certainly not going to start now. He pulled out his phone. She felt her phone vibrate. "I sent you my address. If you show up, I know you felt the same way I did." He walked to his SUV, got in then pulled off.

CHAPTER NINETEEN

There are moments in a man's life when he knows what he has at his fingertips. When the elevator doors opened into his living room, Devin was standing next to the fireplace with a drink in his hand, dressed in grey slacks and a grey and black sweater.

"I wasn't sure you would come."

Ruby stepped inside allowing the elevator doors to close. "I'm here."

He sat the drink on the mantel, walked over to her and removed her purse and coat. He placed them on the sofa then took her hand. They walked through the vast open room from the area designated as the living room by the furniture, to the massive dining room table that could seat at least twelve, turning to the spiral staircase right before they reached the open kitchen area.

He didn't say a word until he reached what she was certain was the opening to his bedroom. He leaned against the doorframe with his arms folded across his chest as she glanced inside.

She leaned against the opposite side with her hands behind her back.

"Once you step inside this room, there will be no games, no doubt, no drama about who I am and who you are to me," he gazed into her eyes earnestly. "Are you ready, Ruby?"

She had never been more ready for anything in her life. "I've never been in a serious relationship. I don't know why," she shook her head. "I just...haven't. I felt that kiss through every pore in my body. I've been going around in circles ever since. I don't know how to love you but, yes, I'm ready."

Devin closed the distance between them until he was merely a breath away. He put his arms around her waist to pull her closer. "We'll go slow, as slow as you need." He put her arms around his neck taking her lips with a softness that almost made her melt, right then and there. He ended the sweet torture by whispering a promise against her lips. "Wrap your mind around the fact that I am going to make love to you tonight."

"What about taking it slow?" she held him close, not letting go.

He slowly pulled her sweater over her head. "We are. We're going to slowly take a shower," he kissed her shoulder. He unzipped her jeans then slowly peeled them over her behind. He unzipped her boots, removed them one at time, throwing them to the side. He pulled her legs from each jeans leg, then sat back on his haunches staring her up and down. "Then I'm going to explore every inch of your body," He kissed her navel. Her body shivered as his hands roamed over her thick thighs, over her panty covered behind, up to her breasts covered in black. He stood and gazed into her eyes. "I promise to go real slow."

Her reaction to his touch was real. The shivers did not give her mind time to think about her body not being a perfect size six. She didn't think about the fact that a man hadn't viewed her naked in years. None of the insecurities she'd been worrying about as she drove to his house came to mind as his hands caressed her everywhere. His touch was electrifying, but that wasn't what ignited her juices to a boiling point. It was his eyes. The way he looked at her as if she was the most beautiful woman in the world. That was what made her forget to be nervous, as she pulled his sweater over his head, throwing it onto the pile he created with her clothes. That was what made her hands roam over his wide shoulders and down his smooth chest. It's what made her kiss his nipples then trace a path of kisses down to the zipper of his pants. She unzipped them, and almost screamed as his manhood escaped, standing at full attention while his pants dropped to the floor. She gazed up at him. "Are you for real?"

He smiled. "I like being free." He stepped out of his pants then stood back. "I want to see all of you, Ruby."

Her breasts rose and fell from the breath she released as she unhooked the front of her bra, allowing it to fall to the floor. She then dropped her panties and stepped out of them. "If I'd known I was going to end up here, I would have worn something sexier." She blushed.

"There is nothing you could have worn that would make you sexier than you are at this moment." He lifted her into his arms. "Wrap your legs around me Ruby."

To her surprise, he carried her into his walk through shower turning on the lower heads as he stood her on her feet. Trails of kisses began at her neck then traveled to her breasts, where he captured a nipple between his lips, causing her to lean against the wall from the sheer pleasure. The warmth and moisture from his mouth, the pleasure from his sucking, caused her to moan. His hand covered the other breast, circling around the nipple, creating different sensations in each breast and causing pressure to build slowly through her body. He switched his mouth from one breast to the other, causing her to cry out.

"Devin." She didn't know if she should pull him closer or push him away. The fear and the pleasure she knew was to come had her conflicted. But he took that away the moment his hands moved to her waist. His lips traveled downward, kissed her navel, then his tongue licked between her thighs. That's when the damn broke. She could feel his smile against her thighs as he took every drop of her, ignoring the sharp cry of release that left her breathless.

He then reached for the free-arm showerhead, replacing his lips with it between her legs, putting it on pulsating mode. He held it in place as she stood and leaned into him. "Ruby, open your eyes."

When she did, he was gazing into them. "The passion in your eyes is the best aphrodisiac known to man."

"Devin," was all she could say as her eyes closed again.

"Let's get this first one out of the way. I'm going to protect us," he said as he replaced the showerhead then reached above her. She heard the wrapper rip. He covered himself, then slid slowly inside of her.

She was wet, tight and hot. He was willing his body to go slow, but her inner walls contracted. Her legs wrapped around his waist pulling him deeper inside.

He groaned, "Ruby," taking her hands into his as he began to move inside of her. The rhythm of their kissing and thrusting merged into one as both became frenetic. The pulsating from the showerheads pounding down on them, added to the heat that was rising, steaming the entire room. Their gasps for air were filling the room and soon turned to her scream of pleasure. The explosion that followed caused Devin to curse.

Devin's body was now crushed against hers. His head was in the crook of her neck. Her thighs still wrapped around his waist, her hands smoothing his shoulders.

"You just made me the proudest man in the world, Ruby Lassiter." He kissed her neck.

She began to laugh. Her head dropped to his shoulder. "I can't believe I just did this."

Devin eased her legs down. "And you find this funny?"

Ruby was still laughing when she looked up at him. "My sister told me to clear the cobwebs from between my legs." She bent over laughing. "Well I would say the cobwebs have been sucked, licked and washed way now."

Devin laughed as he kissed her then licked his lips. "They were rather tasty." He put her over his shoulder carrying her to the blower. Sitting her down, he held her arms up as they twirled around, drying their bodies. The two were like kids in a candy factory. They made love for hours as if they were discovering love making for the first time. When they had no choice but to rest, they lay entwined in each other's arms talking about family. He shared his concerns about his mother being alone. He talked about the responsibility of fulfilling his father's request for Aaron's House and the shock of discovering just how wealthy they were.

"We always lived so modestly." He shrugged as he played with her fingers. "I never wanted for anything. So I see no reason to change the way we live. I think my mother should move."

"Oh no," Ruby shook her head. "Don't mention that to her. There are memories of your father in that house. I just met her, but she shared stories about the two of them with that house as the centerpiece. She's not ready to let that go." Ruby nodded. "When she is, you'll know."

Devin pulled her under him, then settled on top. "How did you learn to read people so well?"

"I have six brothers and five sisters," she was circling the tip of her fingernail around his nipple. "Believe me, I had to learn how to read some of the best minds in the world."

He raised an eyebrow, as if disbelieving her. "I'm serious." She laughed. "You will understand when you meet them."

He smiled. "I'm going to get to meet the family?" He positioned the tip of him at her entrance and slid in. "That means I'm in." He moaned.

Ruby inhaled. "I would say that is a definite yes."

CHAPTER TWENTY

Ruby was in heaven. She was warm and cozy as she stretched. "Hmm," she groaned. Muscles were sore in places she didn't know existed. She pushed her hair out of her face and opened one eye then looked around.

"Good morning."

Ruby rolled over to see Devin dressed and sitting in the chair by the fireplace she hadn't noticed last night. She pulled the sheet up to cover her breasts then smiled. "Good morning," she brushed her hair down with her hands; certain it was wild and all over her head.

Devin loved the sight of her. That's why he hadn't left for work. He had been sitting there wanting to kiss her, but didn't want to wake her. "I've never seen anyone smile the entire time they were asleep."

"How would you know?"

"I watched you. All night."

"Do I snore?"

"No. You do hog the bed," he smiled as he stood. "I have a nine am appointment. Breakfast is in the oven and coffee is ready."

"I don't get a good morning kiss?"

"No...I will not make it out this door if I do that." He smiled. "I needed to see that before I left."

"See what?"

"The essence of Ruby Marie with that after glow from a night of love making."

"You can pat yourself on the back. You left your mark."

"I'd rather pat your back. Have dinner with me tonight at TJ's?"

"Okay," Ruby blushed.

Devin took his suit jacket off the hanger. "I'll pick you up around seven." He was walking out the door when he yelled back. "Your cell phone has been buzzing for the last hour.

"Okay," Ruby ran to the hallway wrapped in the sheet then looked into the foyer below. "Is it okay if I shower before I leave?"

Devin was putting on his long dress coat when he looked up at her. "I would prefer you stay just as you are. But if you have to, I put a toothbrush, washcloth and towel on the vanity. The spare key is in your purse. Make yourself at home."

"My place after dinner?"

"It's a date." Devin smiled then walked out the door.

Ruby stared at the door for a while, then began really looking at his place. "Wow, this is really nice." Not wanting to wear out her welcome, Ruby walked back in the room, took a shower then ventured back downstairs. She was walking towards the kitchen when she heard her phone buzz. Changing directions, she picked up her purse from the sofa and retrieved her phone. "Hello."

"Ruby, are you all right?"

"Hi, Dad," she sat on the edge of the sofa and smiled. "I'm fine. Why?"

"Your mother was concerned."

"Oh Dad," she sighed. "You and Mom need to stop worrying. What are you doing up? Don't you have to work tonight?"

"I'm going to bed now that I've spoken to you. Call your mother."

"I will. Love you."

"Love you too."

Devin walked in singing. "Good morning Mrs. Tally."

"Good morning to you sir." She followed him into the office. "You nine am is waiting."

"Did you have a good holiday?"

Mrs. Tally paused, somewhat surprised by the question. "I did."

"So did I." He hung up his coat. "Thank you. What else do we have today? Anything major?"

"A few in-house. I can reschedule them if need be."

"The need is a be." He laughed aloud.

"All righty then," Mrs. Tally laughed. "Enjoyed your holiday I take it?"

"We should have more holidays."

"You're the boss, make it happen. I'll send your nine am in."

Devin laughed. "Do that and I'll see about those extra holidays."

There was a light knock on the door. "Good morning Mr. Upton. May I come in?"

"Good morning Cameron, please do."

The young woman walked in and took a seat in front of his desk. "Thank you for seeing me on such short notice."

"Any time." He could sense she was nervous. "What would you like to discuss?"

"Sir, I was wondering if it is possible for my position to be transferred to Aaron's House. I spoke with Ruby and one of the main functions she wants in place is an employment mentorship program. That's where we would take each recipient; place them into the Aaron's House program for training sessions to teach how to complete job applications, take standard tests, interviewing skills and how to dress for success. It's really a great program and I would like to be a part of that."

Devin nodded. "It sounds like a good program. You are one of the contenders for a director's position here at Upton. You're willing to give that up?"

"My husband and I talked about this over the holiday. I realize I'm altering my career path. But to be honest Mr. Upton, the people who will be residing at Aaron's House need me. I think I could be of assistance to Ruby as well."

"You like Ruby?"

"Oh yes, I do."

He nodded. "You know I no longer have the final say at Aaron's House. But I will speak with my mother regarding your request on a temporary basis. I think it would be counter productive for you to withdraw from the director's position."

"Thank you, Sir," Cameron stood.

Tania walked into her office knowing she had to keep Jeremy satisfied until she could get him the job. She checked the directory for the warehouse to see who she had to contact to have supplies sent out. She didn't want to go to the person in-charge of the warehouse. That might bring too many questions. She went through the personnel records to see if anyone had been written up for anything she could hold over their head. Less than an hour into her search, she found two. Deciding to go with the most recent offender, she made the call requesting the items, on the list from Jeremy, be mailed out. She gave the young man the address and indicated it should be sent before close of business. Eager to please, the young man confirmed the order and indicated he would get on it right away.

Breathing a little easier now, all she had to do was let the guilt trip she put on Devin at dinner a few nights ago play its way out. As Assistant Director, she felt it would give Jeremy a culprit to blame if anything went awry. She turned on her computer to check her emails. There was one from Miranda stating they were reviving the Christmas party. It would be held in the community center at Aaron's House. This would give the employees at Upton the opportunity to witness the late Mr. Upton's dream come to life. In addition, a new employee incentive program entitled, "Red Slippers" would be initiated. She was encouraging all department heads to nominate an employee within their department for the coveted Red Slippers. She explained further that the selected employee would be granted one wish. The cost of the wish could not exceed $12,000. In addition to bragging rights, they would get to house the encased Red Slippers at their desk for a year. After which time, they would be awarded to a new recipient. The message came with the prettiest red diamond studded heels with a bow on the back.

"Nice presentation," Tania thought. "Who would have thought the old woman had it in her?" then she looked at the bottom of the message and saw, "flyer designed by Ruby Lassiter, Director of Aaron's House." Tania frowned. "Haven't officially started the position and rubbing elbows with the old lady." She huffed. "Don't get too comfortable Ruby. Your days are numbered."

Her desk phone rang. "Upton Investments, Tania Reid."

"Tania, will you step into my office for a moment."

"Of course, Devin." She hung up the phone thinking he must have made a decision regarding the Director's position. She stepped into the hall way just as Cameron walked by.

"Cameron," Tania stopped her. "What are you doing here? I thought you were working at Aaron's House."

"Good morning. I'm sure Mr. Upton will bring you up to date on things. Have a good day."

Tania watched as the woman stepped onto the elevator. Her steps towards the office were a little slower now. Could he have named Cameron to the position? She was definitely screwed if he did. Cameron was as by the book as they come. If she got the position, there would be no more favors. Jeremy could kiss all thoughts about the job good-bye and if he talked, so would she. With that, would go any chance of her breaking free of Jeremy.

"Good morning Tania," Mrs. Tally said as she smiled. "Go right in. Mr. Upton is waiting."

Tania took a deep breath, then walked into the office.

"Good morning Tania, thank you for coming. Have a seat."

"Good morning."

"I would like for you to continue in the role of Acting Human Resources Director for a few more months. I know this is not what you wanted to hear. However, it does give you a longer period of time to demonstrate your abilities."

"I see." Tania inhaled. "You know I will do my best to ensure the progression of the company in whatever capacity you see fit."

"I appreciate that Tania."

She stood slowly. "Devin, I really am good at what I do."

"I believe you can be." Devin sat back. "Our Human Resources Director needs to be fair and impartial. It calls for a bit of empathy with employees. One has to be willing to listen to the needs of others and act accordingly. I'm looking for an exceptional Director from who the employees feel their concerns will be addressed."

"If you don't think I'm that person, why am I still here?"

"I trust my father's judgment. He was considering you for the Director's position because he believed in you. I want to believe in you as well. But there's a side of you hidden from us. I need to know the person I'm placing over the livelihood of five hundred employees. With time, I believe you will trust us the way you trusted my father. However, the question remains. Are you worthy of our trust?"

"I am," she replied.

"You have six months to show me."

Tania knew he was right, but she was not going to trust him or anyone with her past. "I accept the challenge. I'll prove to you that I can be trusted. One more question. Do you want me to close out the Jeremy Claiborne file?"

"What are your thoughts?"

"We could offer him the Assistant Director's position. I'm certain Ms. Lassiter would welcome someone with his skill set."

"Okay" Devin nodded. "On Monday see to it that Ms. Lassiter receives his file. It will be up to her to consider Mr. Claiborne for the position."

CHAPTER TWENTY-ONE

Ruby pulled into her driveway and sighed. There were three vehicles parked there. She knew what was waiting for her inside. She laughed for this is exactly what she would have done if one of her sisters were out of touch for any period of time. "Suck it up." She laughed to herself as she walked up to her front door. The key wasn't necessary. The door swung open.

"Where have you been for the last twelve hours?" Phire, the youngest checked her watch as she glared at Ruby.

Ruby stepped inside and closed the door behind her. "You are letting my heat out."

"Oh, you got some heat all right," Opal nodded with her arms folded across her chest. "It's written all over your face."

"Let's everybody chill for a minute," Diamond stood from the kitchen table where she had been sitting.

"Yes, let's give the harlot a chance to speak," Pearl laughed.

"You still haven't answered Phire's question," Jade added. "You don't have to. But was he good?"

Ruby had to laugh. This is the inquisition she had been a part of in their lives. It was her turn to take the heat and it felt good.

She put her purse on the table, then hung up her coat. She turned to see all five of her sisters' eyes on her. She leaned against the corner entrance into her living room and smiled. "His name is Devin Upton and yes he is very good."

The women laughed, some awed, then another voice came from the kitchen. "You had sex with your father's boss?" Sally held a cup of tea in her hand when she looked around the corner with a raised eyebrow. "Devin Upton is the new CEO of Upton Investments. Your father runs the warehouse for them."

"Dad works at A&M Logistics," Phire corrected.

"I know where your father works. He's been there for thirty years."

"A&M logistics is owned by Upton Investments," Opal stated. "At one time they handled supplies for the company only, but when Upton began purchasing and renovating properties they started a warehouse division."

"And your father has been the only manager they have ever had," Sally stated. "Now when and where did you meet Devin?"

"Upton is the one sponsoring Aaron's House."

"The new job?" Pearl asked as she walked into the kitchen.

Phire turned to Ruby. "Did you have sex with Daddy's boss? Is that where you were last night?"

"Ya'll are freaking me out with the Daddy's boss thing," Jade stated as she sat in the lounge chair with her legs across the arm. "Let's call the man by his name."

"So did you sleep with him?" Phire had her hands on her hips tapping her foot.

All eyes, including Pearl, who was now standing behind Sally eating a bag of chips, were on Ruby.

She sighed. "Yes I did."

"Was he good?" Phire held an eyebrow up.

Sally smiled. "You can see it in her eyes." She sat the cup down. "It's not just sex, is it?" Sally put her arms around Ruby's shoulder.

Ruby looked into her mother's eyes, smiling as a tear fell from her eyes. She shook her head. "No."

"Aww Ruby," Diamond walked over and pulled her into a loving hug. "I'm so happy for you."

"It's a wonderful feeling, isn't it, girl?" Pearl now held a chicken leg in her hand. "Be careful, he will have you barefoot and pregnant once you tell him."

Opal laughed, "You better stop eating like that before you blow up."

Jade walked into the kitchen taking the chicken leg from Pearl as she passed by.

"Hey!" Pearl frowned.

Jade walked back in with an apple. "Eat that," she said to Pearl. "So when are you going to see him again?" she asked Ruby.

"Tonight," Ruby wiped the tear away. "I have no idea what I'm going to wear. He's only seen me in jeans or messed up one way or another."

"We need to go shopping?" Phire walked to the closet and started pulling out coats.

"Where is he taking you?" Jade asked as she took her coat from Phire and put it on.

"TJ's."

All action stopped as eyes landed on her again.

Pearl dropped the apple core in the trash then reached for her coat. "Oh, hell yes. We're going shopping. This one is on me."

"Who's driving?" Jade asked as she walked out the door.

"Everyone can fit in my car," Diamond said as she grabbed her purse and coat.

"I have dibs on the front seat," Opal called out.

"I'm the pregnant one," Pearl yelled, "I get the front seat."

That quickly, the once full, living room was empty and only Sally and Ruby remained standing in the same place.

"So does he feel the same way?"

Ruby started laughing and for some reason could not stop. Sally watched and marveled at the change in her oldest daughter. The look in Ruby's eyes brought tears to hers. It was wonderful to see love in her baby's eyes. She hugged her. "Okay, let's get you a knockout dress so you can really show off those nice legs of yours."

Ruby nodded, "It's funny having the shoe on the other foot," she said as she climbed the stairs to her bedroom.

"Yes it is," Sally called up the stairs, then said to herself. "You have no idea how much fun it's going to be." She put on her coat. "I'll meet you in the car."

Sally got into the back of the SUV.

"Where's Ruby?" Phire asked.

"She'll be right out, she's changing. Ladies, we are declaring this Ruby's coming out day. Any plans you had just got cancelled."

"I have a date with Grant," Opal declared.

"I thought he was just a friend," Jade questioned.

"He is a friend."

"I'm certain Grant will understand, this one time Opal," Diamond said with a smile. Just call him."

"While you are making calls," Sally added. "I want all your brothers here tonight before she goes out on her date."

"May I do the questions?" Pearl pleaded. "Oh, please...allow me."

Everyone in the car was laughing when Ruby got in. "What's so funny?"

"Pearl stopped hating men long enough to get knocked up with twins."

Everyone in the car turned and glared. Phire shrugged. "I'm just saying."

Pearl stared at her mother in shock. It never occurred to her that she very well could have twins.

"Don't look at me like that." Sally laughed. "Twins do run in the family."

Jade and Opal raised their hands. "Double whammy."

Diamond watched the color drain from Pearl's face. "Pearl they are just teasing," she said as she touched her sister's arm. "I did not have twins."

"That's right," Pearl nodded then glared back at Phire for saying such a thing.

"Diamond is right," Phire nodded. "It could be triplets." She shrugged. "I'm just saying."

"Please start this car before Pearl has a conniption in here." Ruby turned to Phire. "One more word and I'm telling everyone what we talked about last week."

Phire slid down in her seat, "I'm glad you are getting some, maybe you will stop taking the fun out of everything."

The shopping trip was fun and a huge success, but Ruby was glad to have a minute alone. Submerged in her soaking tub, she smiled at the memories from the night before. She knew what her heart was telling her, but her mind wanted her to wait. Take some time. Get to know the man before she even thought about love. It had literally only been four days since she first saw Devin. Yet it felt as if he had been around all her life. Then last night, the way he made love to her...she closed her eyes to the memory of his touch, those fingers that caused her body to explode more than once. The way he kissed. Knowing when to be gentle and when to demand what he wanted. Just the thought of it was causing her body to shiver. Shaking off the desire to be with him again, she sat up and began washing. She wanted to have plenty of time for hair and make-up.

CHAPTER TWENTY-TWO

When Devin arrived at Ruby's Condo, he could not park in the driveway because there were so many cars there. He looked around to make sure he was at the right address and then walked to the front door. Before he could ring the doorbell, a man answered the door. Devin raised an eyebrow." Good evening, I'm looking for Ruby Lassiter."

"Are you Devin Upton?"

"I am. And you are?"

"Unimportant until you answer a few questions." The man stepped aside. "Come in."

Devin hesitated. The man was dressed in a suit and seemed to be presentable, however there was a menacing aura about him.

"You are here now, you might as well go all the way in."

"Joshua, step aside," Pearl spoke.

Devin was relieved to see the woman, but still very leery of the man she called Joshua.

"Devin," she held her hand out. "I'm Pearl, Ruby's sister. Come in please." She rolled her eyes at Joshua. "Don't mind him, he's trying to play his brother role."

"Brother," Devin nodded.

"Yes, brother," Joshua replied as he looked the man up and down.

There were more. Devin stopped at the entrance to the living room. Diamond noticed the man's discomfort and stood extending her hand. "Hello, I'm Diamond Davenport, Ruby's middle sister. Let me introduce everyone," she said after he released her hand. "There are quite a few of us so pay close attention.

There were women sitting on the right side of the room and men on the left. As Devin looked around he recognized one.

"Luke Lassiter, running back for the Redskins," Devin grinned then held his hand out as Luke stood.

"Ruby's brother," Luke shook the man's hand.

"Nice to meet you," "Devin replied. Suddenly a pretty young woman appeared directly in front of him.

"Sapphire Lassiter," she grinned brightly up at Devin. "I'm the youngest sister. May I just say you are fine..." She put emphasis on the word fine.

Jade pulled Phire back down in her seat. "Jade Lassiter, Twin to Adam," She pointed behind him. Devin turned to see a tall slim man wearing a fedora hat leaning against the wall at the entrance. He knew the man wasn't there before. The man tilted his hat. "Adam Lassiter."

Devin nodded. "How are you doing?" He was another one Devin did not want to cross, he thought as he looked from the one named Joshua who was leaning against the opposite wall. Devin frowned wondering if they were guarding the door to keep him from running out.

"Don't mind them," Opal stood. "Opal Lassiter, twin to Timothy," she pointed behind him again.

Devin took a deep breath then looked into the kitchen where there were other people.

Timothy walked out of the kitchen and shook Devin's hand. "I'm going to make this a little easier on you." He pointed. "Samuel is the oldest, he pointed to the man with his arms folded standing behind a chair in the kitchen. He nodded. "Joshua is next in line, then comes Ruby, Mathew, Pearl, Diamond, myself and Opal, Luke, Jade and Adam then Sapphire."

Devin listened as he continued to stare at Samuel. "There are twelve of you in all," he started to laugh. He looked around the room and laughed again.

Adam and Joshua shared a glance. "Harvard has figured it out," Adam said with a smile.

Devin shook his head as he began to remove his gloves. He pointed to Samuel, "Your father wouldn't happen to be Big Joe, would he?"

"We just call him Daddy," Mathew said from the kitchen.

Devin could not stop laughing. "Ruby is Joe's daughter." He shook his head in disbelief.

Joshua nodded. "Impressive Harvard," he pointed in the kitchen. "Take a seat."

"I'll take your coat," Diamond held out her hand as Devin, removed his coat.

Samuel patted the back of the chair. "You're in the hot seat."

"Okay," Devin walked by everyone then sat in the chair. He took a deep breath as he took in the entire Lassiter crew. "Joe has an impressive family."

"Flattery is not going to get you anywhere," Pearl waved him off. "We have been waiting years to get back at Ruby. So here's how it's going to go. "We have five questions; two from the gents and two from the gems. I hold number five."

"Okay," Devin clapped his hands together. "Shoot."

Joshua pulled out his gun. "Okay."

"Whoa..." Samuel stood in front of Devin. "You hurt him you will have to deal with Ruby."

"You don't want to deal with Ruby now that she is getting some," Phire huffed. She looked around at the glares. "I'm just saying."

"There is a time and place to say things Phire," Jade scowled at her. "You 'just saying' isn't going to work much longer."

"So stop and think before you speak," Opal added.

Devin still had his eyes on Joshua. He was fairly certain no one in Joe's family would harm him, but then again, Joshua looked like a loose cannon.

"You all right in there, Harvard," Adam grinned.

"I'm good," he didn't sound so sure. "What are the questions for?

"To determine if you are worthy of dating our sister," Luke explained.

"You see," Pearl spoke up. "We are a close knit family. We have each other's back on all fronts. It is important for you to understand what comes along with dating a Lassiter."

Devin smiled. He liked the idea of knowing Ruby had a family who loved and cared for her. "All right," he started to say shoot, but thought better of it. "Ask away."

"After raising us, Ruby may not want to have children," Opal started. "But if she did, are you able to get it up, knock the cobwebs out, cause it's been a while for sister girl and what are your thoughts on children?"

Devin thought, sat back and crossed one knee of the opposite leg. "I rise every time I see or think about Ruby."

"I can see that," Phire nodded.

Devin sat up, in an attempt to hide his arousal. "How old are you?"

"Old enough to know better," Samuel glared at his little sister.

"I'm just saying...." The others said along with her.

"We know," Opal frowned at her.

"Continue Devin, please," Pearl instructed.

"Cobwebs were cleared out last night. As for children, I would love to have one or two."

"Twins run in this family, my brother," Luke grinned.

"Thank you for the warning. Next question."

Timothy spoke. "I like to ensure my sisters are financially stable. You are in investments. We have good and bad days. If you had an opportunity to purchase stock with Apple, a well-oiled institution, or buy with a startup for pennies on the dollar what would you do?"

"It's depends on the startup." He sat forward, very comfortable with the question. "You see people tend to jump at a recognizable name, but that stock will cost you a pretty penny, and nine times out of ten it's not going much higher. With the right start up, you could buy one hundred shares at five dollars. It would cost you five hundred dollars. With the well-known stock, you might get about five shares. You may earn a few dollars when it's time to sell, but not much more because it has reached its peak. The lesser known stock is a little different. In a year or two, the stock that you purchased for five dollars could be selling at one hundred dollars a share and moving up. You would have more than tripled your initial investment."

"Wise advice," Timothy nodded.

"Only you would get that," Mathew teased.

"No, I get it too," Opal, added.

"I got it," Adam acknowledged.

"Okay, back to you," Jade sat up. "You can take care of her financial needs. And according to you the physical needs are met. What about the needs of the heart? Do you have anything in your background that would prevent you from giving Ruby your all when it comes to love? Because she deserves nothing less."

"No baby mama drama. No crazy ex-wife, girlfriend or anything that I am aware of. However, life is unpredictable. I can't promise nothing will creep up. But if it does, it will be handled."

"Good honest answer," Diamond nodded. "I like him."

"You like everybody," Phire smirked.

"Yes, you do, Diamond," Pearl, agreed.

Adam stepped forward. "We believe in protecting our sisters. It is important to us to know who ever is in their lives can protect them with the same vigor as we. If confronted, are you capable of protecting her?"

"You touch what's mine and I will kill you. We can discuss the reasons later when I join you in hell for taking your life."

Joshua and Adam held up their hands. "He gets a ten." Adam reached out and gave Devin a pound.

"That's right," Joshua cheered. "Take him out. You can ask questions later."

Devin held up his hand. "Let's see if I can save you some time and concern. In my eyes Ruby is a precious gem. One any man would be fortunate to have. I'm blessed because she chose me. Most men aren't at a point in their lives to recognize something so rare when it is placed before them. I am not most men. I have waited a lifetime for Ruby. I would have to be a fool to let her get away. A fool I am not." Devin looked around the room at each of them. "I will treat

Ruby well, because of the queen she is. Not out of fear of you," he looked at Joshua, "or for the love each of you have for her." He stood, "I've enjoyed this. Now, if you all don't mind, I have a date with a woman named Ruby."

Pearl put a hand on his chest. "Wait, not so fast." Devin sat back down as she bent over and looked into his eyes. "Ruby is the oldest of the gems. She raised all of us in one way or another. We are who we are because of her. She never asked for anything in return." A tear dropped from her eye. "I need to know you will love and cherish her for the beautiful woman she is."

"Pearl."

Everyone looked up to see Ruby standing in the middle of the floor.

"Wow! Look at you," Phire cried out. "Aww man, you getting some tonight."

Ruby grabbed Phire's ear. "Watch your mouth."

"Ouch," Phire pulled way. "I'm just saying you look good."

Ruby smiled. "Thank you," she turned to find Devin standing next to her.

"Hello beautiful," he pulled her into his arms and kissed her as if they were alone in the room.

Timothy held up his card. "Ten."

Mathew was next, "Ten," he nodded.

"Ten? That man deserves twenty for that bold move," Luke laughed.

"I'm with you," Jade gave him a five. "He's not joking with that kiss."

"All right," Sally said from the doorway, "You two get out of here. It's beginning to snow again and you don't want to get stuck here with all of us."

Devin heard that and ended the kiss. "Let's go," he whispered to Ruby.

Samuel held Devin's coat, while Pearl held Ruby's.

"Take care of her," Samuel patted Devin on the shoulder.

"Have fun Ruby," Pearl kissed her cheek. "You do look good."

CHAPTER TWENTY-THREE

The Christmas holiday season was in full swing as Devin and Ruby stepped out on the town with dinner, the theater and snowball fights with the family. Joe and Miranda were surprised to learn their children were falling in love.

"Aaron would have been over the moon about this," Miranda said as she watched the snowball fight from a window in Sally's home.

"Yes, he would have." Joe laughed. "We always talked about me having so many children to his one. He said that one brought him more joy then all twelve of mine put together. We used to fight over that one."

Sally gave Miranda a cup of hot chocolate. She sat on the arm of the chair Joe occupied just as a snowball hit the window.

Miranda jumped.

"That window has been broken many times from footballs and basketballs. Believe me, a little snowball doesn't stand a chance against it."

They all laughed as the girls tackled Devin to the ground. Luke picked them off one at a time.

Devin got to his feet, swiped Ruby up in his arms and carried her off the field.

"It's been a long time since I've seen this side of Devin."

"It's good to see Ruby so carefree."

"He's a good man," Joe said as he smiled at Sally.

"How is Aaron's House coming along?" Sally asked.

Miranda's eyes lit up. "You should see what Ruby has done with that place. The apartments are finished and ready for the first occupants to move in. She has selected five families so far with another five waiting for approval. Your daughter has an amazing spirit."

Devin and Ruby stomped the snow off their boots at the door then walked inside.

"Time to go get the trees," Ruby announced.

"Trees," Joe asked. "How many trees do you have to get?"

"Three," Devin replied.

"One for the center, one for Mother's house and one for me."

"Oh, I don't need a tree," Miranda waved them off.

"Yes, you do need a tree," Sally said with a smile. "Joe has to go to work. I can come by to help you decorate it."

"I lost Aaron around Christmas two years ago and last year I spent Christmas at Devin's."

"Well, you're getting one this year," Ruby turned to Devin. "Let's go before it gets too dark."

"Miranda call me when you are ready," Sally said as she closed the door behind them.

"Mom," Phire called through the door. "We are going to help Devin and Ruby with the trees."

"Have fun," Sally smiled as she waved to them.

Joe walked up behind her circling her waist. "Are they all leaving?"

"Mmm hmm," she waited until the last person was in a vehicle then turned in her husband's arms. "Now we can go have some fun."

"Come here woman," Joe gathered her in his arms and carried her up the stairs.

Tania made it an early day. There was Christmas shopping to be done before she went home for the holidays. The last two weeks she'd had meetings with a number of employees and was doing all she could to help those with concerns. She stayed away from Aaron's House and that seemed to have made a difference with Miranda. She seemed nicer over the last few weeks. Maybe it was because her baby boy was in love. Yes, everyone around the office were talking about the new director and the difference she had made in Devin. "Happy for them," she said to herself as she walked through the parking lot.

"You won't be happy for long."

Tania jumped at the voice. "Jeremy, what is wrong with you walking up behind me like that?"

"You've been avoiding my calls."

"I have no reason to talk to you anymore. I sent the supplies you needed and gave your resume to the new director. I told you after that I was done." She pulled away from him.

"I didn't get the supplies." He grabbed her arm. "If they don't show up by the end of the week, I'm out."

"Why are you tripping? Get the job I set you up for."

"The bitch sent me a dear john letter."

"Well, I'm sorry. I did all I could Jeremy." She walked way.

He grabbed her and pushed her against the car. "You're going to get me into that warehouse. I can't lose my job right here at Christmas. I go down, I'm taking you with me."

"How am I supposed to get you into that warehouse? I don't work there."

"It's your company's warehouse. Call them. Tell them I'm picking up something for you."

"Then what?" she snatched away, "You're going to bust your way in and take what you need?"

"Don't you worry about that, just call them."

Tania made the call. "This is it Jeremy. Brother or no, I'm not doing this again. You can tell anybody you want about my past. I don't care anymore." With that she walked away and did not look back.

The midnight shift was short tonight. Joe had given some of the men time off for Christmas. There were a few special orders that needed to be pulled and shipped out before the holidays. He would get those done and out of the way tonight. That way, when they closed for Christmas Eve the guys would be free for the rest of the year. Any orders coming through after tonight, would be filled and shipped at the beginning of the year. Bonuses would be good this year for the workers. They all had done a great job. He had even put in a few names for the Red Slipper incentive. They were going to tease any man who won, but he thought it would be fun.

Walking through the door, he noticed that a pallet stocked with boxes of supplies was near the loading dock. He wasn't aware of a pickup for tonight.

"Hey Lance," he called out to one of the workers.

"Hey Joe. It's going to be a quiet night."

"Looking forward to it. Do you know anything about this order?"

"There's a note stating it was to be picked up tonight."

Joe looked at his watch. "After midnight?"

Lance shrugged his shoulders. "I don't know."

"Okay," Joe glanced at the order then went to his office.

A few hours later Joe and Lance had pulled the special orders. They were preparing shipping labels when they heard the dock door go up.

"Anybody else scheduled to come in?" Lance asked.

"I gave the men this Friday off."

"Oh, but you made me come in."

Joe laughed as he walked to the front. "You think I want to be here all night by myself?"

Two men were standing at the dock loading items from the pallet Joe questioned earlier.

"How you doing?" Joe asked.

The two men stopped and stared up at the six-eleven man.

"We're good, sir," one man replied. "Just picking up this order for headquarters. We didn't get it last week. So I had to come out here tonight and get it to them by morning." The man threw his hands in the air. "You know how it goes."

Joe nodded, but knew something wasn't right. "I've been wondering who the order was for." He walked over to the desk near the door where the sign in sheets for pickup were located. He reached under and pushed the security button. "Give me a name so I can check it off." He took the clipboard and turned to see a gun pointed at him.

"Anybody else in here?"

"Man, put that away. We don't need that." One of the men yelled.

Joe held his hands up as he walked backwards to the opening. He did not want Lance to walk in on whatever was happening. "No, It's Christmas. I'm the only one here." He yelled hoping Lance would hear him.

"Get out the way. Do you see how much stuff is in this warehouse Jeremy? Man we could clean up right here, tonight. I got babies looking for a good Christmas."

"Joe?" Lance called out.

Joe turned just as the gun sounded. "Run," was all he could get out before the felt the heat of the bullet hit his head. He fell to the ground and his world went black.

CHAPTER TWENTY-FOUR

The telephone ringing in the middle of the night is never good. Two ringing at the same time is devastating.

"Hello."

"Speaking," Devin listened as the officer on the phone spoke. He pushed the sheet aside and stood just as Ruby's cell phone buzzed. His eyes honed in on it willing it to stop buzzing. It was almost in slow motion as he watched Ruby's arm come from beneath the sheet reaching for the device. He heard her say hello. Then he watched as she sat straight up in bed.

"Phire, calm down." She looked at her phone. It was 2:47am. She put the phone back to her ear. "Who's in the hospital?" The line went dead.

Devin was dressed in sweats and held a pair out to her. "Get dressed babe."

She held the phone in her hand dazed as Devin pulled the sheet off her. "Put your feet in."

"Let me call my Mom."

"No," he shook his head. "She's at the hospital," he said as he pulled the shirt over her head.

Ruby shoved her arms through the sleeves. "Why is my Mom at the hospital? Why is Phire crying?"

Devin grabbed her hand. "My Dad," a now panicked Ruby asked as she grabbed her phone understanding the urgency now.

"Something happened at the warehouse," Devin said as they ran down the stairs. He shoved his feet into a pair of boots, grabbed hers then pulled her into the elevator. She held on to his shoulders as he put her boats on. He stood.

Ruby saw the frightened look in his eyes. She wasn't sure why. "What happened to my father Devin?"

He took in a deep breath. "He was shot during a robbery attempt at the warehouse."

Ruby simply stared at him. She began shaking her head. "No." She shook her head again. "No." The question clear in her eyes.

"I don't know, Ruby." Devin's heart was breaking for her. "I don't know." He pulled her into his arms and held her.

They rushed through the doors of the emergency room stopping at the intake desk. "Joe Lassiter."

"Trauma two, follow the yellow line."

Devin grabbed Ruby's hand. Looking at the floor he turned the corner following the yellow line.

"Ruby," Phire jumped into her arms crying.

Ruby consoled her little sister. "Phire, it's going to be okay. I'm going to talk to Mommy."

Phire shook he head. "She's not talking Ruby and no one will tell me anything."

Ruby kissed her forehead and hugged her. "I'll find out what we need to know." She gave Phire to Devin, then walked over to her mother.

The woman who always seemed like a little giant was sitting in a chair against the wall. Her eyes were staring straight into a room where a team of doctors and nurses could be seen through a window.

"Daddy," Ruby sighed quietly as she took her mother's hand. She closed her eyes and prayed. First for her father, then for her mother. Then she asked God to give her the strength to help her family get through this.

She opened her eyes to find her mother staring at her. "Mom, what happened?" that's when tears began to stream down her mother's face. No words came out as her mouth moved. "I'll find out Mom. Don't worry. Daddy is going to be fine. I'll make it right." Her mother squeezed her hand, but still did not speak.

"Phire," she called out.

"Yes," the young woman sounded scared. "I need you to sit here, hold Mommy's hand and talk to her. Just keep talking okay."

"Okay, Ruby. I can do that."

Ruby smiled. "I know you can."

Devin stood back and watched Ruby literally transform. She walked to the nurse's station. "Excuse me. That is my father, Joseph

Fitzgerald Lassiter. Would you give me an update on his condition?"

Mathew and Timothy walked around the corner. They spotted Devin and turned towards him. From the look on their faces he knew all hell was about to break out.

"Where is he?" Mathew was yelling. "Where is he?"

Ruby turned as the nursing staff looked at the men who had just arrived. "Excuse me," she said then stepped over to her brothers.

"Matthew, your father was shot. Your mother is close to being in shock. I need you to be strong for them. Do you hear me Matt?"

The angry face seemed to have melted away as he reached out and grabbed his sister.

"I know, Matt, I know." Ruby hugged him. "Will you call Jade for me?"

"Of course," Matt stood straight, wiped his face dry then pulled out his cell.

Ruby turned to Timothy. She reached out and touched his cheek with the palm of her hand. "Will you call Opal?"

Timothy hugged her. "You got it."

Devin started to say something, but she held up her hand. "I can't fall into your arms right now. My family needs me. Will you try to find out what happened?"

"I will," Devin squeezed her hand giving her a moment of comfort. She slowly pulled away then walked back over to the nurse's station.

"Will you please contact your administrator?"

"It's three o'clock in the morning ma'am. He's not here."

Ruby took a deep breath. "Who is your supervising nurse?"

"Mrs. Atchison."

"Will you get her please?"

"She will tell you the same..."

"Get her now," Ruby's voice rose a notch or two. "I'm sorry. This hospital is about to be invaded by the likes of people you cannot imagine. I'm struggling right now. Because that man is not only my father, he is the father of a CIA agent, and the Press Secretary for the President of the United States. As I said, you are about to be in hell for the next few hours or more. Will you please call your administrator?"

"Nurse Atchison, report to trauma one, Nurse Atchison report to trauma two." Was heard over the loud speakers.

Ruby smiled. "Thank you." She stepped away then dialed the number she knew would get everything in motion. She took a deep breath. "Pearl, Daddy's been shot. He is at Regional Medical."

"What's his condition?"

She had to form her lips to say it. "Grave."

The silence on the other end of the phone spoke volumes. She hung up just as Diamond turned the corner with her husband Zackary.

"Ruby?"

All Ruby could do was put her hands to her mouth to keep from crying out.

Diamond took off her coat, then removed Ruby's. "You take the guys. I'll take the girls."

Ruby nodded.

"Excuse me."

Ruby turned.

"I'm Nurse Atchison. The White House has contacted our administrator with instructions for your family. Your sister and brother are being flown in. They should arrive in about forty-five minutes. Do you have the authority to make decisions for your father?"

"My mother does." Ruby replied.

"Okay," Nurse Atchison held her hand. "Here's what I know. They have stopped the bleeding. The bullet entered the left side of his head then exited near his temple. They began performing surgery immediately upon his arrival."

"What are his chances?"

Ruby looked over her shoulder to see all of her siblings who were present standing behind her, except Phire who was still clinging to her mother's hand.

"That, I don't know. As soon as I know, the information will be relayed to you. For now he is still alive."

"Thank you," Ruby exhaled then turned to them. They all looked to her expectantly. "Daddy is holding his own for right now and we need to do the same thing." She nodded. "Sally loves him too. She needs us right now. Daddy is in the surgeons' and God's hands."

"What in the hell happened?" Luke walked up behind them.

"Devin is trying to get details," Ruby guided them to the side of the room away from Sally. "As soon as he knows he will let us know."

Jade ran around the corner. She stopped when she saw everyone gathered. Tears swam down her face as if a water fountain had erupted.

Ruby gathered her in her arms. "He's in surgery. We don't know much more than that right now." She stepped back giving her a slight smile then looked around at everyone in the area. "Where there are two or three gathered in my name."

"I am there among them," Matthew added.

The family gathered around holding each other's hands. Devin, took Ruby's hand, she held Sally's who held Phire's, Zack took Diamond's, Grant took Opal's, Timothy took the other, Jade, Mathew and Luke completed the circle. They began with the Lord's Prayer.

CHAPTER TWENTY-FIVE

They all knew the moment the choppers landed. Secret Service agents filled the room first. Walking briskly through, securing every corner of the building. The agent in charge was pointing out areas to place agents. Pearl appeared first with her husband Theo who was once on staff at the hospital. He walked right over to the nurse's station.

"Who's doing the surgery?" Nurse Atchison pulled him aside as they went over the chart.

Next came Samuel and his wife Cynthia. "The Chief of Police is supposed to meet us here. Has he reported in?"

Ruby nodded. "He's talking with Devin." Samuel stormed away.

Cynthia looked at Ruby. She kissed her cheek then went to sit with Sally. Diamond held on to Ruby's hand.

"Joshua and Adam are here," Jade closed her eyes.

Ruby looked around. "How do you know?"

"I can feel Adam's anger."

They saw Amber before Adam. She went right to the nurse's station and took them through the same questions that Theo had.

"I hope Adam marries her," Jade squeezed Ruby's hand. "She keeps him grounded."

A doctor came out with Joshua walking behind him. The man did not stop where the crowd now stood. He went straight to Sally. He glanced at Joshua who gave a curt nod. "Mrs. Lassiter I'm Dr. Patel. Your husband is out of surgery. There is some damage. The extent cannot be determined at this time. For now he remains in critical condition."

For the first time in hours Sally stood. "Thank you, Dr. Patel." The doctor was hesitant to move. Sally tilted her head at her son. "Joshua."

He raised an eyebrow at her. "He's free to go."

Dr. Patel did not hesitate, he quickly moved from the middle of the family.

Sally looked around at all of her children and their spouses. "Where are my grand babies?'

Everyone started talking at once explaining where the babies were.

Ruby eased away from the group to stand back and breathe. The sun was coming up behind her as Devin walked over to her. He pulled her into his arms, put her head on his shoulder and allowed her to finally release her own tears.

Devin watched as all the family turned to them. Sally walked over first. Devin opened his arms to welcome her in. Soon the entire family was in one big hug. That is until a hand reached inside, pulling him out.

Samuel, Joshua, Adam and Luke stood there staring at him. "You know someone named Jeremy Claiborne?" Samuel asked.

"Names sounds familiar," Devin thought for a moment.

"Jeremy Claiborne?" Ruby walked over. "He applied for a position at Aaron's House."

"That's right he did. He was the other applicant for your position."

"What does he have to do with this?" Ruby asked.

"That's who the police have in custody." Luke stated.

"Lance said your father jumped in front of him," Devin added. "So he didn't see who took the shot."

"Who is Lance?" Samuel asked.

"He works with Dad," Adam stated as he worked on his laptop.

"Did you locate them?" Joshua asked.

"Got them," Adam replied as the two began walking away.

"Roc is going to be upset if you get hurt, Joshua," Ruby called out.

"Let them do what needs to be done," Samuel said to Ruby. "How do you know this person?"

Ruby shrugged her shoulders. "He applied for the Assistant Director's job." She turned to Devin. "Tania brought me the application. She said it came from you."

Devin shook his head. "He applied for your position. When I hired you Tania requested he be considered for your assistant position."

"Did she have something to do with this?" Ruby asked.

Adam came back through the door. "Devin, did you know that Claiborne is the half-brother to one of your employees? A Tania Reid." He nodded. "According to these records Claiborne has had a pretty good side line going on kickbacks on supplies ordered for different facilities."

"I'm going to kick her ass," Ruby walked briskly past Adam.

"Ruby," Devin called out.

Samuel stopped him. "No, you should wait."

Seconds later, Diamond, Opal, Jade, Phire and Pearl were following her down the hallway.

Theo ran, grabbed Pearl and turned her around. "Oh no, you don't."

Ruby had no idea who was in the car with her. All she knew was she was going to whip Tania's ass. She pushed the speakerphone in Devin's car.

"Cameron," Ruby called out. "I need Tania's address, now."

Cameron who was clearly still asleep mumbled something unintelligible into the phone.

"Cameron wake up," Ruby yelled.

"Ruby," the woman sounded awake now.

"Yes, I need to know where Tania lives."

"You sound upset. Is everything okay? Why are you calling from Devin's car?"

"Too long of a story and no, Cameron it is not okay. I should have kicked her behind the first day I met her."

"Sending her address to your cell phone right now. Do you need me to meet you?"

"No, I have all my sisters with me."

Cameron laughed. "Can I just come and watch."

Ruby hung up the phone. "I'm going to jail today."

"We're going with you," Phire huffed.

Ruby's cell phone buzzed twice indicating there were two text messages.

Phire checked her phone. "We got the address, twice." We should use the one Adam sent."

"Why?" Jade asked.

"It has the code to her alarm system."

"Good," Opal added. "Save me the time from having to figure it out."

None of the ladies thought twice as they knocked on the door of Tania Reid. "Open the door or I will kick it in." Ruby yelled.

Tania opened the door with a multicolor scarf around her head and a robe she was pulling together as Ruby punched her dead in the face propelling her backwards.

"What the ..."

Before Tania could say another word, Ruby was on top of her punching her again.

"Who in the hell are you people?"

Ruby looked up to the staircase. "Mr. Dance?"

Cecil Dance was standing there with pants unzipped and no shirt on. "Ms. Lassiter, what are you doing here?"

Opal and Jade pulled Ruby up by the arms.

"Kicking Tania's ass." Ruby scowled down at Tania who was making every effort to get up and out of arms reach. "Her half-brother had my father shot last night trying to rob the warehouse. How did he get in Tania?"

"I don't know," she wiped blood from her nose. "And I don't know anything about your father being shot."

"Joe," Cecil came down the stairs. "Is he...?"

"Barely alive," Ruby cried. "If my father dies..." she wiped tears from her eyes. "I'm going to come back and send you to hell."

"We have a report of a disturbance," an officer said from the doorway.

Phire smiled at the young officer. "There is no disturbance. My sisters and I were just being a little rowdy," she giggled. "We'll keep it down." The women all stood in front of Tania. Ruby had a death grip on her neck as the officer looked around.

"Sir?" The officer questioned Cecil.

"They will be fine." Cecil walked to the door, half way closing it. "They play rough all the time."

"The vehicle is parked a little haphazardly," the officer stated still not certain all was well. "You could get a ticket for that."

"I'll take care of that," Phire stepped outside with the officer. "The keys are in the car."

Ruby turned to Tania and pulled her up from the floor.

"I didn't know about your father."

Cecil turned to Ruby. "Her brother has been blackmailing her to do things she really didn't want to do. I will take her to the station to make a statement to the police." He helped Tania up. "And she will tell the truth, all of it. Right Tania?"

"All of what truth?" Ruby asked.

Hesitantly, Tania spoke. "Jeremy knew how I paid my way through college. He was threatening to tell everyone about it."

"So?" Opal looked at the woman questioningly.

"Oh, I get it," Jade smirked. "You made your living the old fashioned way."

Ruby looked from Jade to Tania, then it dawned on her. "You're a hooker?"

"Was," Tania huffed.

For the first time in days, Ruby's laugh came from her rib cage. "For all your talk about degrees and fitting into Devin's world, you earned your living spreading your legs." Ruby shook her head. "I'll be damned." She turned and walked out of the apartment followed by her sisters.

By the time the girls made it back to the hospital, Joe had been placed in a private intensive care room with around the clock nursing staff. Amber and Theo assured them that everything that could be done for Joe was being done. But there was no way to predict what the outcome would be.

Visits were limited to two at a time and only fifteen minutes for each. As word spread about Joe, the number of family and friends increased

It was almost midday, when Joshua and Adam returned. When they did, Samuel walked off with them to a corner in the waiting room.

Devin placed Ruby's now sleeping head on Diamonds arm then joined them. One by one, Zack, Grant and Theo did the same.

"Did Claiborne confess to the police about shooting Joe?"

"He told us everything we needed to know before they took him to the hospital," Adam replied.

"Hospital?" Devin raised an eyebrow. "I didn't realize he was injured."

"He wasn't," Joshua replied. "He is now."

"It will take as long for him to recover as it will take my father," Adam added.

Ruby glanced at the men talking and knew whoever hurt her father was now dead or in a hell of a lot of pain. She sighed, then looked at Opal. "Grant is fine."

"Yes he is," Phire mumbled in her sleep.

Opal smiled. "We're just friends."

"With benefits," Phire yawned as she turned over "I'm just saying."

CHAPTER TWENTY-SIX

A week had passed and with each day there was improvement in Joe's condition, but he had not opened his eyes or given any sign of consciousness. Sally spent every day and night at his side. So did each of his children. They took turns at being in the room with Joe and Sally. The boys would come in and play cards with Sally, or fill her in on the craziness of their lives. Mathew was taking it the hardest. He would come but not be able to stay long. Seeing his father lying still was killing him inside. Luke would come and move Joe's arms and legs around to keep him flexible, he said. Adam and Timothy would have conversations with Joe as if he was advising them. Joshua would pray with Sally to keep her spirits uplifted. But it was Samuel who kept Sally smiling. Phire would lay beside her father and talk the whole time she was in the room. Jade would read one of her stories to him. Opal would calmly explain why Grant was just a friend. Diamond kept him abreast of the baby news and Pearl just complained about the world in general.

Ruby, well, she filled her time simply holding his hand. Taking joy from feeling the strength and heat it generated each day.

Devin, he was the rock she never had before. Each day Ruby would go to Aaron's House, move a family in, set up all their services, then go to the hospital to be with her family. At night, she would go to Devin's place to cry. He would hold her through the night, then make sweet love to her each morning. She had no idea how she would have gone through this alone.

"You will never have to go through anything alone again." He would say. "I am here with you."

It was the night before Christmas Eve. The employee party and grand opening of Aaron's House was that evening. Ruby was torn when she woke up that morning. She reached over to his side of the bed but he wasn't there. Pushing her hair from her face, she sat up and looked around. He must be downstairs, she thought. Going through her morning routine, she took a shower, washed her face, brushed her teeth then headed downstairs in a pair of sweats, a tee shirt and bare feet.

The Christmas tree they'd put up the night her father was shot was in the corner as pretty as ever. It brought forth her second smile of the day. Devin brought the first. That morning after they made love, he discussed the situation with Tania. He decided she was not the best fit for the Human Resources position, but felt she was a victim. He allowed Ruby to decided Tania's fate. She surprised him with her decision. Ruby

thought Tania should work on the Red Slipper
Incentive Program to improve her people skills.
In addition she had to volunteer twice a week to
work at Aaron's House, reporting directly to Mr.
X. That was about all anyone would be able to
take of Tania at the facility.

Walking down the stairs still admiring the
tree, she heard her mother's voice. Was she
crying?

"Mom," Ruby rushed down the steps.

"Hey," Sally hugged her daughter. "What's
wrong? Did something happen?"

"No," Sally rubbed Ruby's arm to calm her
down. "I came by to see you."

"I can get dressed and go to the hospital with
you."

Devin walked by and kissed her on the cheek.
"I'll be upstairs.

"Okay," Ruby said as she watched her
mother.

"Devin came to the hospital this morning to
ask your father for your hand in marriage. He
told him, he would wait until he was able to walk
you down the aisle."

"Devin did that?"

Sally nodded. "Yes, he did." She fought back
tears. "He loves you so much Ruby. And I'm not
going to answer for your father. We're going to
wait until he can tell Devin yes." She pulled out
a tissue to wipe her nose. "I want you to go to the
party tonight. The girls have picked a beautiful
dress for you. Miranda has something special
planned for your father. You have to represent
him."

"Mommy I don't want to go to a party while Daddy is..."

"Ruby Marie Lassiter you are going to do this for you father and for me." She kissed her daughter's cheek. "Now, Phire is waiting in the car to take me back to the hospital."

"You're letting Phire drive?"

"Yes, it's time for her to grow up."

"Take plenty of pictures," Sally ordered as she put on her coat and scarf. "I'll see you tonight and tell me all about it."

Ruby watched her mother walk out the door. She went upstairs and found Devin sitting in the chair in front of the fireplace. He had made the bed and a beautiful red gown was lying across it. She felt the smooth material and marveled at the red diamond heels next to it.

"The dress is from your sisters. The shoes from Pearl."

Ruby laughed as tears rolled down her cheeks. Devin held his hand out. She took it, sat beside him and marveled in his warmth. "Your father told me once, I would find the right gem to light my way. He was right. I found a Ruby and now I can't imagine my life without you." He kissed her temple. "I know deep down you have an old fashioned family. So I'll do things the old fashioned way. I asked your father. As soon as he gives me an answer, I'll ask you."

"What happens if he can't answer?"

He held her a little tighter. "Oh, he will. I believe, he will."

EPILOGUE

"Good evening one and all," Miranda began as all the Upton employees and new residents of Aaron's House gathered around the stage with the huge Christmas tree as its backdrop. "What a wonderful way to celebrate the season, families finding new homes. Employees gathering together to share some cheer." She paused. "Two years ago around this time I lost the love of my life Aaron. Tonight I am channeling him to be my angel. I know this is a joyous occasion, but someone we all love is in need of prayer. There are approximately three hundred of you here tonight. If you all would form circles and join hands." Miranda watched as people began to join hands. "Ruby, you come up here with me."

She squeezed Devin's hand. "I can't," she mumbled. "I'll breakdown."

"And we will be there to pick you up." He took her hand and walked her up to the stage. Mr. X who was one of the maintenance people for the building made his way to her. The young boys from the shelter and their families were there. The veteran and his family and others, all formed a circle. The lights were lowered, allowing the tree to illuminate the room.

"Father," Miranda began. "I need your help tonight. Would you send Aaron to talk with Joe? His family needs him to come back to them. Don't take him away from this wonderful family you gave him. I believe this is why you took Aaron. For this very moment, you knew he would be needed. Put him to work tonight. Tell him Devin and I love and miss him dearly. But it's time for him to earn his wings. Send Joe back to us. Let us say the Lord's prayer together."

The room filled with voices as tears rolled down Ruby's face. She wasn't alone at all. Every person in that room was there in prayer with her. Her heart was so filled with warmth, she cried out. But the prayers did not stop. They continued to flow.

At the hospital, Joshua was sitting with his father as Sally read a scripture from the Bible. Phire came running into the room.

"Roc," she was pointing.

Sally looked at Joshua, then back to Phire. "What are you doing?"

Phire ran over and grabbed Joshua's hand pulling him from the chair just as Roc appeared in the doorway.

"This is coming out of me tonight."

Joshua jumped up. "The baby?"

"No, the damn Easter bunny. Yes, the baby."

"Mom, I got to go." He kissed her cheek. "Dad the baby is coming." He stopped to see his father's eyes on him. "Dad."

Sally looked over and gasped. "Joe," she cried. And asked someone to get the nurse. "Joe" she touched his face as a teardrop fell to his cheek. "Joe," she smiled, then gently kissed his lips.

"Daddy," Phire stood behind her mother,

The nurse came in checking his vitals. "Mr. Lassiter," she held a light to his eyes. "Welcome back. Can you blink for me?"

Joe blinked his eyes and Sally cried more. "That's good Joe."

"Do you know who this pretty lady is?"

Joe smiled. He licked his lips. "My sweet Sally," he whispered.

"How did you luck up and get such a pretty one," Dr. Patel asked as he rushed into the room.

Joe looked up at Joshua. "Josh,"

"Joshua your father wants you," Sally moved aside.

Joshua put his ears down to his father's lips and listened. He nodded his head. "You got it."

"What?" Phire asked as Joshua left the room.

"I'm going to have a baby."

Dr. Patel nodded to the nurse. "Will you get them down to obstetrics? We are going to have two miracles on this day. What do you say about that Joe?"

"Sounds good."

Sally broke down and cried.

Back at the center the prayer circle had just ended when Devin received a call. He looked at Ruby and smiled. "He said yes."

"Who said yes?" Ruby asked as she wiped tears from her eyes.

He waited for her to look at him. "Your father. He said yes."

"Okay," Ruby replied as she began gathering her things. "I want to go back to the hospital now to check on Dad. Mom was right. I needed to come here tonight." She kissed Devin. "Thank you for bringing me. I'm going to say goodbye to the families. Will you get our coats?"

"Yes dear," Devin replied.

"Very funny," Ruby laughed.

It was a joyous sound to Devin. It was the first time she had really laughed since that night. "She's a gem," he heard a voice say. But when he looked around he only saw Mr. X.

"Did you say something?"

"No, I don't even like you."

"I remember," Devin said then smiled. "Merry Christmas Mr. X."

"What did you say to Mr. X to make him smile?" Ruby asked as he held out her coat.

"I asked him how he was going to be a maintenance person if he is half blind."

Ruby looked over her shoulder at him. "You did not?"

"It's a valid question," Devin laughed as he held the door for her.

Twenty minutes later they walked into the hospital to a crowd of people greeting them. Adam and Amber, Zack and Diamond, Theo and Pearl, Samuel and Cynthia, Opal and Grant, Jade, Mathew, Timothy, and Luke

"Hurry Ruby, the baby is coming." Phire grabbed her and started running through the crowd of people.

"Wait," Ruby pulled back as she looked around. "Why is everyone here?"

Pearl, looked at Devin. "You didn't tell her?"

"I did," he nodded.

"Tell me what?"

Sally stepped outside the room and took Ruby's hand.

Ruby walked into her father's room to find him sitting up, looking right at her. Ruby fell to her knees next to his bed putting her head on his hand...

"Daddy," her eyes filled with tears as he gently rubbed her head.

"My precious Ruby." Joe whispered.

Devin knelt beside her holding her as she cried.

"The baby is here." Phire yelled to everyone.

"Baby?"

"Joshua's baby is here. It's a boy."

"Sally go," Joe said. Sally shook her head "Go." He repeated.

"I'll stay Mom," Ruby stood with Devin's help.

Sally kissed Joe then hesitantly followed the rest of the family to see the baby.

"Joe," Devin spoke. "I love your daughter."

"Which one?" was his weak response.

They all laughed, even the nurse who was in the room. "There are many."

"Your first gem. Will you give her away to me?"

"No," Joe then smiled. "I'll share her with you."

Ruby read the card on the bassinet, born at 12:01 am on December 24th, Joshua and Rochelle welcomed their baby boy Joseph Adam into the Lassiter family.

"It's Christmas Eve," Devin smiled at the baby, then turned to Ruby. "It's time to go home."

She smiled brightly at him. "It's time to go home."

They walked outside the hospital at close to three in the morning.

"It's a good night to make love in front of the fireplace."

"I like that idea," Devin kissed her hand. "It's snowing again."

"Oh no. My shoes are going to get messed up." Ruby reached down to take them off."

"You planning on walking in the snow barefoot?"

"It's better than messing up my shoes."

"Hold on to your shoes." Devin picked her up in his arms and carried her to the car.

"I love you Devin Upton."

"I know," he grinned.

"Aren't you going to tell me you love me?" Ruby frowned.

Devin unlocked the car with the key fob then opened the door. Once she was seated, he took her shoes and placed them on the dashboard. Getting down on one knee in the snow, he reached into his pocket and pulled out a diamond solitaire ring, surrounded by sparkling rubies.

"I love you Ruby Marie Lassiter. Will you do me the honor of becoming my wife?"

At three o'clock in the morning, with snow falling around them, tears fell from Rubies eyes. "You really want to marry me?"

"Yes," Devin replied, "Red slippers and all."

Made in the USA
Middletown, DE
20 May 2024

54583870R00093